Dedication

To all my friends and family who have encouraged me to keep writing, especially Hester Goddard, my best critic, who set me on the right track with this book.

R.J. Sloane

Confessions of an Heiress

AUSTIN MACAULEY
PUBLISHERS LTD.

Copyright © R.J. Sloane (2016)

The right of R.J. Sloane to be identified as author of this work has been asserted by him in accordance with section 77 and 78 of the Copyright, Designs and Patents Act 1988.

All rights reserved. No part of this publication may be reproduced, stored in a retrieval system, or transmitted in any form or by any means, electronic, mechanical, photocopying, recording, or otherwise, without the prior permission of the publishers.

Any person who commits any unauthorized act in relation to this publication may be liable to criminal prosecution and civil claims for damages.

A CIP catalogue record for this title is available from the British Library.

ISBN 9781786295033 (Paperback)
ISBN 9781786295040 (Hardback)
ISBN 9781786295057 (E-Book)

www.austinmacauley.com

First Published (2016)
Austin Macauley Publishers Ltd.
25 Canada Square
Canary Wharf
London
E14 5LQ

Chapter 1

My name was Annabelle, the same as my mother's. And that was about all I was sure of anymore. When it happened, I think I grew up very suddenly: one moment I was an innocent child, albeit not a happy one, and the next I was an uncomprehending adult.

My mother had called me into her bedroom where she was getting ready to go to one of her boringly interminable galas, or whatever they were. It was a Friday evening, and it also just happened to be my sixteenth birthday. I had been showered with presents as usual, none of which I really wanted or needed, not even the beautiful, white Palomino pony which was now safely locked away in the stable block. However, I hadn't had a party, which was all I really wanted – to dance to loud music with kids my own age. But, as I'd never had a party, I hadn't really expected one.

I knew when I first entered her room that she'd already had a drink too many and I wondered what I was going to get scolded for this time – an invisible stain on my spotless dress, perhaps?

She sat me down on the chaise longue and promptly plonked herself down next to me. This was unusual in itself and I wondered if the scolding I was expecting was to be more serious than I'd thought. What had I done which was so bad recently? I racked my brains but could come up with nothing concrete – a few peccadilloes, that's all. My marks at school, as usual, were not spectacular but not bad either. Then she took my hand. This was absolutely unheard of. My mother *never* touched me!

She said in her low, husky, supposedly sexy contralto, 'Darling, I think you're old enough now to hear the truth.' What truth? I didn't want to hear any truths, thank you very much. I already knew about the birds and the bees from school, although admittedly only in theory. *She* had certainly never told me! I pulled away from her and looked into her slightly drunk eyes – my eyes too, as it happens, exactly the same shade of brown flecked with green.

'I have never told you about your father, have I?' she enquired, almost querulously. I'd always been told that he'd run off with one of the chamber maids when I was tiny and had accepted this as the truth. But was this truth an *un*truth? I wasn't that bothered actually, although occasionally I felt a pang of regret that I'd never had a male figure in my life. After all, most of my school friends' parents were either now on about their third marriage, or were single parents like mine. And the rest of them were clearly sleeping around from what their kids said. It didn't exactly engender confidence in me about the state of marriage. I suspected my mother had had many lovers but had always assumed her one true love had been reserved for my errant father and that was why she'd never married again.

'What about him?' I said abruptly.

'Well, the fact of the matter is...' And here she inhaled deeply and paused as if not knowing how to continue.

'Oh, do spit it out, Mother!' I cried in frustration.

'Well, the fact of the matter is,' she repeated and I wondered just how drunk she was and if she was ever going to get to the point. But then she said, almost piteously, 'You don't know how difficult this is for me, darling! But I'm determined to tell you, so here goes. You're old enough now.'

She took a deep breath and continued. 'Well, before you were conceived, I was getting very broody and, as I didn't have many child-bearing years left to me, I desperately wanted some sort of human legacy to leave behind. However, there wasn't anybody I liked well enough to marry and I was determined to keep my independence. So I decided that the best way forward would be to obtain some sperm and have my baby artificially conceived.'

I was listening to all this with growing horror and broke into her monologue to exclaim, 'So I was an IVF child!'

'Yes, I'm afraid so,' she continued, unperturbed. 'One of the first, actually. And just to make doubly sure, I used two lots of sperm from two different men at the same time, both of whom I knew quite well and liked. And, lo and behold, it worked! So, I actually have no idea who your father is.' I sat there, stunned. Then she continued, 'I'm sure you'll want some proof of what I'm saying.'

And at this point she rummaged around inside her handbag and brought out a piece of paper and handed it to me. I had never seen my own birth certificate and I looked at it curiously. I saw my name and date of birth at the top and then lower down under "father's name", it just said baldly, "father unknown". Then the implications of what she'd said hit me and I burst into tears.

'That's disgusting!' I said, sniffling and thinking how loveless and cold my begetting had been.

'Maybe to you now,' she replied, 'but one day, if you're ever in the same position as I was, I'm sure you'll understand. Anyway, I guess you want to know why I've decided to tell you now.'

I just nodded mutely and she went on, speaking sadly now, 'The fact of the matter is that both the men whose sperm I used are now dead. One of them died a few years ago in an accident and the other very recently of natural causes. So I felt you deserved to know that you are definitely fatherless now.'

'Thanks a lot!' I cried bitterly.

'But at least I've got a lovely daughter out of it all!' Mother concluded with a flourish, smiling now as if waiting for applause.

'It's too much to take in all at once,' I said then, through my tears.

My mother murmured, 'I know, dearest one, but you will come to terms with it. I know you will.'

And with these words she picked up her coat and walked, as straight-backed as a soldier, out of the room and down the stairs to the car where her chauffeur was waiting patiently. I took a few deep breaths, hoping to calm myself down, but then ran back to my own room where I flung myself on my bed and wept bitterly for my lost innocence.

Eventually, however, my tears dried and I started to think more rationally about my situation. What would my friends at school say if

I told them I was an IVF kid and not even my mother knew who my father was? 'That's horrible!' is what, and I wouldn't blame them a bit. And I didn't know anybody else to tell. Did the servants know? I guessed probably not. It must have been a closely guarded secret between Mother and her doctors.

That thought led me on to consider "Mother" in more detail. What did I really know about her and my dysfunctional, so-called "family"? I knew now, just as I'd always known subconsciously, that I had always been a kind of trophy for her, somebody she could show off as an extension of herself – witness the way she insisted on my having exactly the same haircut as hers to emphasise how much alike we looked. I knew also that she had never loved me for myself – witness, again, the lack of physical contact between us. I'd had nannies when I was very young who used to cuddle me but now I had servants, a very different kettle of fish. But perhaps the biggest problem of all was that she'd never been there for me when I'd needed her. She'd always been either working, usually in London at the headquarters of her company, or out "having fun" as she called it.

She'd always spoiled and mollycoddled me but now it felt more as if I'd been cocooned or swathed in bandages from head to foot like some kind of Egyptian mummy. I suddenly realised I was a prisoner in my own home and I honestly didn't feel I was exaggerating. This was clear to me from the fact that none of my school friends had been allowed back to the house; not for years.

'They are not *our* kind of people and, anyway, they're too noisy,' Mother had said once and I'd believed her. Not "our kind of people", even though I went to an exclusive school?! But that was exactly what it was: "exclusive", i.e. excluding normal people, the like of whom I'd never met and who, at this rate, I was never likely to meet. I'd never questioned this before but now I had reason to question everything about my existence. I know all this seems rather muddled, but I felt all muddled. And I also felt that all the money spent on me was to buy my silence about Mother's awful secret.

What about my so-called "family"? As far as I knew, it consisted of exactly one person: Mother. I'd never met any aunts, uncles or cousins. I knew she was enormously rich – money she'd inherited from her father, some kind of big-wheel financier – and that I would be an extremely wealthy heiress one day. But so what? I wasn't really interested in money, was I? No, I really didn't think I was. I decided then and there that, when I inherited, I'd give the whole lot away to the most worthy causes I could find. Then perhaps I could find out how ordinary people lived. The only problem with that idea was that it could be years away. Mother was as strong as an ox.

So what about me? Was it, in fact, so awful to be an IVF baby? No, not really. I knew there were plenty of them around. But I suspected that very few of them had been born with, not one, but two potential fathers and that thought made me wonder how she'd managed to convince her doctors to go ahead with it if, indeed, she'd used doctors and hadn't just done it all by herself. But then I remembered her money and its power.

Could I tell her I needed counselling? At least if she accepted the idea – and it was a very big 'if' – I would be able to talk to somebody. But she didn't believe in psychiatrists, saying they were all quacks. And, an even bigger question, why did adults have to impose their own problems, fantasies, etc. on their kids? Surely we have every right to be protected from them? There were too many questions and not nearly enough answers. And even the answers I had were mainly guesswork, except about the money, of course.

I reckoned it was time for an act of pure rebellion. Could I run off with one of the gardeners à la D.H. Lawrence, or join a commune in San Francisco? No, neither idea was remotely feasible; the gardeners would run a mile if I made a pass at any of them – they were all terrified of my mother – and, at the moment, I had no money to go to San Francisco. I had to wait until I was eighteen for my allowance to kick in.

Wait a minute! What about murdering my mother? Now that was an idea. It would certainly get rid of the central problem and leave me with the money to do what I wanted. Unfortunately, however, I knew nothing about the practicalities of murder. I didn't even know how to find a hitman to do the job for me and, anyway, I'd surely get caught and be forced to spend the rest of my life in prison and I didn't fancy that at all.

Then I had another idea. I had a mate at school who I was pretty sure fancied me. What about eloping with him and running off to Las Vegas or Gretna Green or somewhere to get married where they didn't ask questions? But again there was an insuperable obstacle in my way. Although I liked the boy, I certainly didn't love him and even more certainly didn't want to have his babies.

That seemed to leave only one option – to meet someone completely new with whom I could fall in love and run away. But how on earth was I supposed to meet such a mythical creature? Then it struck me like a thunderbolt from the Gods. I could get Mother to take me to some of her galas! There I could certainly meet somebody, surely? Admittedly they were all rich, these so-called "friends" of Mother's. But I had nothing against money per se. It was just that I didn't want it for myself.

So I made a decision. Soon I would start asking her to take me to some of her wretched galas or charity do's or whatever she called them. If I was old enough to be told such news, I was certainly old enough to go with her. She would probably resist at first but I would persist and finally she would give in.

But that was a long-term decision. What about in the short term? Then I remembered an earlier thought about appearance. I could change my looks! All I needed was a stout pair of scissors with which to hack off my mane of auburn hair and some dye (preferably green) to change its colour and I would no longer be recognisable as my mother's daughter. Brilliant! That decision also made, I was finally able to sleep.

Chapter 2

A short time later I did what I'd decided and changed my appearance dramatically. I now looked like a Goth with dyed black hair, which was about as different from my mother's demure look as it was possible to get, much to her annoyance. I even had a nose ring inserted and a couple of small, discrete tattoos inked on! She threatened me many times with all sorts of awful punishments but, apart from locking me in my room for a while after each new shocking transgression, nothing much had happened.

We'd not spoken again about the central issue of my father and I suspected that she now regretted our little chat and hoped I'd forgotten all about it.

However, after much pestering, she finally agreed to take me to one of her gala events, saying that she supposed it *was* time to introduce me into "polite" society, but she absolutely insisted that I undo all the work I'd done on changing my appearance. And reluctantly I did this, except for changing my punkish hair style, as I simply could not bear the thought of going as my mother's clone. I did, however, have to change it back to its original colour. We argued about the hairstyle for ages but I wasn't going to give way and finally, after an exasperated, 'You're so obstinate!' she let me keep it.

So there we both were in the Daimler or Rolls, or whatever it was, being whisked across the city to its biggest museum where the occasion was to take place. I knew my mother was a big patron of it and fervently hoped that some of the other patrons there would have brought their kids along. She'd told me in no uncertain terms that, if I didn't behave myself, she'd have absolutely no qualms about having me ejected, forcibly if necessary, and I had meekly agreed to her terms, being really excited about the possibility of meeting some new people, preferably boys, who might be sympathetic to my plight.

Mama was dressed to kill in a long, black Viacci evening dress, dripping with diamonds, while I'd foregone my usual look, comprised of sneakers, ripped jeans and t-shirt with no bra and instead was wearing a brand new longish blue dress with little puffs on the sleeves and new slingback shoes. I felt like a character in a nursery rhyme picture book. Mother had failed to notice the small flick knife I'd put in my purse along with the can of Mace I always carried. Just in case, I'd told myself. In case of what, I had no idea.

You can imagine my horror when we turned up and I met the other guests of the museum on that evening. They all seemed to be about ninety-five and none of them had brought their kids (or grandkids, even). I was the only young person there by about sixty years!

When we all sat down for dinner, I was seated next to an ancient old codger who at least had a twinkle in his eye when he looked me up and down. We chatted a little before his dragon of a wife made him talk to her. He was a bit deaf which forced me to speak rather loudly and I blushed when, during a pause in the general conversation around us, I could be clearly heard delivering some kind of inane opinion about local politics. Mama turned from her neighbour and gave me a disapproving frown. But, unfortunately, it wasn't a bad enough sin to get me ejected, which was all I really wanted at that point.

Things brightened up when the soup came, though. Our table was served by a dashingly handsome young man who winked at me when he served me. I blushed again which made me extremely cross with myself but I managed a polite smile back. The other courses duly came and went and I said nothing to anyone else during the dinner. We all had wine to drink but I was only allowed a couple of glasses when all I felt like doing was getting extremely drunk.

Then it was time for the speeches and I managed somehow to sit through my mother's, which was the first, without falling asleep. However, I knew that I'd go completely mad if I had to undergo any more and whispered to her, when she returned to the table, that I needed to go to the bathroom.

So I tiptoed to the back of the huge hall, looking for the usual sign but not seeing it. Just then, the handsome waiter who had served us came out from what I presumed was the kitchen and noticed me standing there, looking a bit lost.

'Can I help you, Miss?' he asked and I told him I was looking for the bathroom. 'Follow me, Miss,' he said unhesitatingly. So I did.

We walked for what seemed like ages through musty-smelling galleries, all empty at the moment, until finally we arrived at a door with the familiar image on it. We said nothing to each other on the way but I liked the way he moved, striding along in front of me. He had a nice arse, I thought. There he turned to me and said, 'Here we are. I'll wait outside. Don't want you getting lost on the way back, do we?'

'Thank you,' I said weakly and went in. I had a quick pee and you can imagine my astonishment when I came out of the stall and found him preening himself in the mirror, right there in the ladies' toilet!

He turned and said, 'All done, are we?' I was at a complete loss for words and just stared at him.

I instantly spotted the big lump in the front of his trousers and knew that he wanted me. The trouble was that I wanted him too. I know I should have grabbed my purse, which I'd left sitting on the long counter in front of the mirror, taken out the Mace and given him a good squirt but I didn't. I felt like a rabbit trapped in a car's headlights and could only stare, transfixed. He looked back at me with his large, long-lashed, black eyes and I was lost.

Then he came up to me and gently stroked my hair. I put my head on his shoulder and he drew me close. Then in one swift movement he picked me up, turned around and put me down on the counter. Smoothly he pulled up my dress, pulled down my knickers and took out his penis, which looked enormous and purplish in the harsh, overhead, fluorescent light.

'No,' I whimpered, but he paid me no heed and proceeded slowly, ever so slowly, to push it inside me until it was all the way in. Fortunately, my own juices were flowing freely well before then, otherwise he probably would have found it much more difficult to penetrate me fully. The pain was excruciating at first and I cried out but then, quite quickly, it became exquisite. Even after he (and I!) had come, I was still moaning with pleasure. 'Do it again, please!' I pleaded, but he shook his head saying, 'Your mother's probably wondering what's become of you. You have to go back.' And I knew he was right. I also knew that, technically, I'd just been raped, but I didn't care.

Then I looked down at the inside of my thighs and saw quite a bit of blood. Oh no, that's torn it, I thought. But immediately I realised the pun and started giggling inanely. I must have been in shock. 'What's so funny?' he said but, when I didn't answer and just continued giggling, he must have noticed the blood, for he said, 'I'll help you clean that up.'

He went and got some paper towels from the dispenser, soaked them in water and proceeded to wipe the inside of my thighs with them until the blood had disappeared. After that he dried me off, his hands feeling deliciously erotic against my skin down there. I could feel myself coming again now and didn't resist it. He needed to wipe me once more after that.

'What's your name?' I whispered.

'There's no need for names really, is there?' he said.

'No, I suppose not,' I replied. We walked back together to the banqueting hall with me hobbling a bit. 'How do I look?' I asked at the door.

'Fine,' he said.

I knew my cheeks were burning but I pushed open the door and hurried over to my mother's table. She didn't even turn to look at me and, for once in my life, I was grateful for her lack of attention towards me. I sank into my seat, had a big swallow of some kind of liqueur and waited for my breathing to return to normal. I didn't listen to a word of the rest of the speeches but just sat there, dazed but happy. We finally returned home late and there I was, having been relieved of my virginity. What an extraordinary evening!

I knew two things for sure now: first, that I was a fully-fledged woman and secondly, that I wanted more of what the nameless waiter had given me. I didn't *think* I was a nymphomaniac, but I didn't care. But how was I to get it? I'd dropped my plan of going to more of my mother's wretched galas. Apart from the incident with the waiter, they were just too boring and I rated the chances of meeting him again as less than zero.

Fortunately, my period arrived on time. I'd been very worried in case he'd impregnated me as I certainly didn't want to go through the hassle and ignominy of an abortion. That would have given my mother an even greater hold over me. So I knew I had to think again. However, I had no idea what other alternatives were open to me.

Needless to say, I told nobody about my adventure in the toilet, especially not my school friends. The girls would just have giggled and asked me for all the gory details while the boys would have considered me a tramp and probably tried to use me as one.

Chapter 3

I'd been studying hard for the past year and nothing particularly dramatic had happened. My dreadful mother had still not said another word to me about my father. It was now only a few weeks until my eighteenth birthday and I knew that once that day had come and gone, Mother would have no more hold over me. I'd be free to do as I wished as I'd have my own money and I couldn't wait for the day to arrive. Incidentally, I'd been manless since my humble waiter and I fervently hoped this was about to change.

So I'd been planning feverishly. I knew I wanted to go to university and, indeed, had been encouraged to do so by my teachers. That seemed to be the obvious way out. My marks had got better and I'd applied to several of the best universities in the country without telling my mother; she would surely have thought of some cunning plan to dissuade me. So I played the perfect daughter, even to the extent of letting my hair grow back until it again looked much like my mother's. I didn't do this out of any feeling for her but simply because I knew that the punk look would probably not go down too well at uni.

What was I going to study? Psychology was the answer, as I wanted to find out more about my mother's mental state – and, incidentally, my own – and to see if there was any way in which I could have her institutionalised or even put in prison for the psychological damage I felt she'd inflicted on me, although, of course, I didn't put that on any of my application forms.

Then one day I got the e-mail I'd been waiting for. I'd been accepted provisionally by most of the colleges I'd applied to! So now I had to make a choice. And my choice was based on geography. I would go to the university furthest away from home, in Aberdeen, way up in the north of Scotland. So I e-mailed them a letter of acceptance, knowing that in the autumn I would be able to start a whole new phase of my life.

***

Well, my birthday has come and gone and what an awful, terrible day it's been!

It started as all my other birthdays have started, i.e. with many of my mother's suitors and hangers-on turning up and giving me innumerable, very expensive presents. I somehow managed to say my thank yous, even if it was through gritted teeth rather than with a genuine smile. Then in the evening came the obligatory banquet, which again I sat through, making all the right noises. Finally, when everything was quiet, I told Mama that I needed to have a word with her and she took me into one of the formal sitting rooms and plonked herself down on a sofa, a bit drunk as usual. I'd rehearsed the speech many times in my head but, when it came to it, I just blurted out.

'Mother, I'm off to university very soon.'

This did not elicit the reaction I expected. She just said, 'I'm sorry, but you can't go.'

'Why on earth not?' I exclaimed, getting angry with her already, as I always did when we talked. 'I'm eighteen now and I've got my own money so I can damn well do as I wish.'

'I'm afraid not,' she replied calmly. 'Sorry I didn't tell you, but I've enrolled you at a finishing school in Switzerland so that you can learn how to become a proper lady and have changed the terms of your allowance so that you can't access the money until you're twenty-one.'

'What?' I screamed. 'Why the hell did you do that?'

'I thought you weren't mature enough yet to have control of so much money and anyway I can't do without you for three whole years.'

'Ah. Now we come to it. You want to keep control over me forever. Is that it?'

'Not at all, Annabelle. It just happens to be the truth.'

Then I burst into tears. I simply *couldn't* go to a finishing school to learn deportment and how to cook crepes. And I most certainly did not want to be forced to become a "proper lady"! But I was still determined to win this argument. So I dried my eyes. 'You do know that Switzerland is a long way away, don't you?' I said.

'Yes, but it's only for a year and I'll see you during the holidays and most weekends, I hope. Anyway, I'm having someone I can trust to keep an eye on you there.'

'You mean *chaperone* me?!' I screamed, bursting into tears again.

'Now, now, darling, don't cry,' she said. 'You know how much it upsets Mummy.'

That made me even angrier. 'You really are a manipulative bitch, aren't you?' I sobbed. 'I don't need your stupid money anyway. I'll get a scholarship.' This only occurred to me on the spur of the moment but it seemed to throw my mother.

'Don't you dare!' she shouted.

'Just wait and see,' I shouted back and flounced out of the room. I went up to my own bedroom, locked the door and lay on my bed, weeping. Why did she always have to ruin everything? But then I remembered that I was now an adult and tears wouldn't help. I needed to do some more planning.

***

After that last, extremely distressing, talk with Mother, I kept out of her way and to a large extent managed to avoid her completely which seemed to suit us both. She, I presumed, was doing all her usual things and I just hoped she wasn't plotting any other gambits to wreck my life with. Meanwhile, I went ahead and applied for a scholarship to the university, citing abject poverty as the reason. But, apparently, they had to do a means test of my parent(s) to see whether I was eligible! This was something I hadn't foreseen. So I knew I had to forget that. I wondered if my mother had already found it out.

But there had to be other ways of getting money, surely? I knew I wouldn't be allowed to work while I was at home so that was no good. Then I had an idea. I could steal some of Mother's valuable jewellery and pawn it! This seemed to be much more promising. I knew she wouldn't miss a few gems. I had a few good pieces of my own as well.

So I went into her bedroom one day when I knew she wouldn't be around, and opened her safe with trembling fingers. I knew the combination from having watched her do it so often, although I didn't think she realised that. Rummaging around in the back, I found a few old pieces that looked valuable but I knew she never wore, and I took them out, putting them in a little velvet bag. Then I hastily withdrew and skipped happily back to my own room. The first part of my plan had gone without a hitch. I didn't feel like a criminal at all. After all, I was just taking what was rightfully mine.

The next day before school I told the chauffeur who drove me there not to bother coming at the usual time to pick me up as I had a band rehearsal, but to turn up a couple of hours later. I sometimes had these rehearsals and he suspected nothing. Then after school I went straight into the city on a bus, which in itself was quite an adventure for me. By asking around, I soon found a small pawnbroker's and went in, clutching my little bag of gems which I'd taken to school that morning.

Inside I showed them to the pawnbroker and he examined them minutely through a magnifying glass while I got more and more impatient. Finally, he looked up at me and asked, 'Are these stolen, by any chance?'

I blushed but replied in my haughtiest tone, 'No, sir. They are not. They are mine to do with as I wish.'

He quailed a bit at my tone but then said, 'I only asked because they are very valuable and you are quite young to be their possessor.' I repeated that they were mine and he sighed and said, 'Okay. I'll give you £20,000 for them,' which sounded to me like a tremendous sum of money.

'Done!' I said and shook his hand.

Then he opened a safe behind him and counted out a seemingly vast quantity of bank notes. When he handed them to me, I thanked him, perhaps a bit too profusely, and he said, 'Look after the money now, won't you? I would hate it if you got mugged in the street.' And I promised I would, stuffing the money into my school rucksack which was almost empty. Then I ran out of his little shop and started looking for a taxi. One soon came and I gave the address of my school to the driver. We got there without incident and I paid him with one of my new bank notes. A little later my chauffeur duly turned up and drove me home.

The next problem was where to hide the money until I was ready to leave home. I hadn't thought about this beforehand. Nosey maids were always coming into my room and I certainly didn't want any of them finding it. Also Mama would come peeking around in there occasionally and I remembered well one occasion when I'd borrowed a pornographic magazine from a boy at school and the row that ensued. Naturally, I didn't have a safe like my mother where I could put the money. That just about ruled out my room. I also knew that there was no way I could take up a floorboard or two, like in some of the crime thrillers I'd read, as they were all solid oak and, anyway, I didn't have the tools.

That left the rest of the house. It was a vast place with many potential hiding places but I finally decided on one of the attics where nobody ever went and where I used to play by myself as a child. So, making sure nobody was around, I crept up there and found it undisturbed, just like I remembered it. I ended up hiding the money at the bottom of an old trunk full of antiquated clothes that, when I was a child, I used to occasionally enjoy dressing up in. By the time I went back to my own room, I was well pleased with my day's work.

Chapter 4

Well, would you believe it! I am now happily ensconced at university and have started my course. Hopefully, my wretched mother won't be able to find me here, although I'm not at all sure about that. I am living in a big house with a number of other students and have had to learn rapidly to look after myself without any help from maids or servants. I have even learned to cook! Only simple things, it's true, but adequate for my needs. I have my own room here, which is light and airy and next door to me there's another girl, called Emma, whom I like. So everything's hunky-dory at present.

How did I get here? That took as much planning as my other schemes. I knew I had to slip away but how could I do it without being seen? In the end, however, it was relatively straightforward. Having received my A-level results, which, by the way, were excellent, one evening after dinner I went up to my room and packed a few essentials into a small travelling case. I knew that I wouldn't be able to carry much with me. Obviously I couldn't take my desktop computer but I remembered to include my precious memory sticks which had my diaries on them and other pieces of my most personal work, knowing that one of the first things I'd have to buy up north would be a laptop. At the same time, I ostentatiously left my mobile phone on my bedside table to let my mother know that I was uncontactable. Then I went up to the attic, taking my school bag, got the money out of the trunk and packed it all away in the bag. I hoped that I'd have enough to be able to buy everything I needed when I got to the university but I didn't know much about money, having never been given much, just a little pocket money, and I didn't really know the prices of things.

Then I waited until everything was dark and quiet and slipped out of the house, remembering to disable the alarm on the way. After that, without a backwards glance, I walked down the long driveway to the electrically-operated gates, opened them with the combination I had remembered from closely watching my chauffeur and walked out boldly into the street, not forgetting to lock the gates behind me. Nobody shouted or came after me and it was with a tremendous sense of freedom that I ran all the way to the railway station which wasn't far away.

I'd checked the times of the trains beforehand and one came quite quickly and, having bought a ticket with some help from a rail employee, I got on it and was quickly whisked to the centre of London. There I had to wait until early morning for the first train out in the direction I wanted to go and I sat in an all-night café at the mainline railway station watching the people. It was fascinating for me to see "real" people for almost the first time in my life and I struck up a conversation with a nurse who was travelling in the same direction as me, although she wasn't going so far.

When the early morning train arrived, we both got on and I left London without a backward glance on the first big adventure of my life. I had to change trains twice more to get to my destination and, by the time I arrived in the evening, I was feeling very tired. But my spirits were high and I took a taxi to the university where I met a few students drinking in the bar. I asked them where I could crash for the night and they were very surprised at my question, asking why I didn't have pre-arranged accommodation. I told them that I was a new student who had only just been accepted and that I hadn't had time to do it. This seemed to satisfy them and one of the girls said I was welcome to use her floor, which was fine by me.

So she took me to her room and I crashed out, only waking at ten o'clock the next morning to find the room empty. It was one day before term was due to start and I knew I had lots of sorting out to do. So, after a quick shower, I took my few possessions (and the money, of course) and hurried over to the main university administration building.

There I presented myself with all my documentation and was formally enrolled. I asked about somewhere to live and was sent to a different department who were very helpful and that's how I ended up in this house now.

So far everything has been fine; I like my teachers and (most of) my fellow students and am enjoying the studies. The money I have would seem to be enough for a while at least but I know that I'll be able to find a job to supplement it when I run out. Only one thing mars my happiness: the thought of my mother frantically scouring the country for me, finding me and dragging me back, kicking and screaming, to my prison. Unfortunately, I'd had to use my real name to enrol and I knew it wouldn't be that hard for anybody to track me down.

Chapter 5

For the past year or so, I've been very busy with my studies and socialising and nothing really dramatic has happened – except with my love life, but I'll try to get to that later.

However, just this morning I had some terrible news: one of my mother's doctors called me, proving, I presume, that they and she have known all along where I am. That was the first thing I thought when he introduced himself and that was bad enough. But there was worse to come. He asked me to return home urgently as my mother's kidneys were failing and she needed a transplant. And, obviously, as her only relative, I was by far the best match. I suspected immediately *why* her kidney had failed. It was all the heavy drinking she'd done ever since I'd known her so, to my mind, it was entirely her own fault.

But, of course, it wasn't quite as simple as that. I couldn't just say 'no way' to the doctor. I was in a state of shock and thought it easiest to simply hang up the phone when he'd finished speaking. He rang back immediately but I didn't answer that time and just let it keep ringing until he finally gave up.

After the call, I realised I had to do some serious thinking. My first thought was that my mother must have planned for something like this to happen when she got ill. She was certainly, in my eyes at least, evil and manipulative enough.

My second thought was: why can't she go on kidney dialysis like everybody else until a suitable match turned up? I knew how Mama would feel about that – helpless and afraid – exactly like I'd always wanted her to feel. So I was tempted to call the doctor back and recommend that course of action, however awful he thought I was. But then again, she was my mother, wasn't she? She'd brought me into the world, however unconventionally, and in the end I owed her *something* for doing that, didn't I? After all, I reckoned I could live with only one kidney.

It was all much too confusing and I had no idea what to do. Then I thought of the university counselling system, which had a pretty good reputation among my friends, a few of whom had been persuaded against suicide by it. However, I'd never been to it myself and was loath to expose all my family secrets to a complete stranger. After all, that was one reason why I was studying psychology: so that I could heal myself. But I knew it was the sensible course of action and at last decided that, yes, I'd give it a go.

***

I have just returned from a lengthy session with a counsellor. Fortunately, it was an older woman; I don't think I could have handled a man. I started by swearing her to secrecy and she pointed out that everything said in her office was completely confidential, like with a priest or a doctor, unless I gave her permission to disclose anything to the relevant authority, and I had to be content with that. I think she probably thought that I was yet another silly girl who'd got herself pregnant and didn't know where to turn.

So that little issue cleared up, I started talking. I began by telling her about my family money and she just lay back in her chair with her eyes closed, but when I got to the bit where I described how my mother had had me, she opened her eyes wide and looked at me piercingly. But she didn't interrupt, although I knew I had her full attention by then. I continued by relating the circumstances of how I'd found this out and went on to describe the awful relationship I had with my mother and the things she'd done to me, including trying to stop me going to university. I concluded by telling her how I'd managed to get the money to come and, finally, about yesterday morning's phone call which had upset me so much.

'That's quite a story,' she said after I'd finished speaking.

'If only it was just a story,' I replied bitterly.

'And now you don't know what to do and you'd like some advice. Is that it?'

'Exactly,' I said.

'Well, the first thing I'd like to say is how brave you were in breaking away from your mother. It must have taken a lot of courage.'

'I'm not sure if it was courage or plain desperation,' I said.

'Yes, I see your point. But I think it shows that, when pushed, you are able to take important decisions by yourself without help from others, although I realise too the difficulty of your current situation. So what are your options?'

'It seems to me that I have only three: either to go home and give her one of my kidneys as she wants, or to say 'get lost' to her, or to recommend to her to try kidney dialysis until the right organ comes along. There are major problems with all of them, however.'

'And what would they be?'

'With the first option it would mean giving in to her again, which I've sworn never to do, and probably missing out on the exams at the end of the first year here if, indeed, she ever allows me to come back. If I just tell her to get lost, she would probably come up here herself or send people up and make a huge scene, possibly even going so far as to offer the university a massive sum of money to persuade me to go home, which they wouldn't be able to refuse. And the third option would probably have the same outcome as the second.'

'I see you've thought this through carefully.'

'Well, what do you expect? It's my life, isn't it? It's all I've been thinking about for the past twenty-four hours!'

'I've thought of another option, actually. What about if you insist, before you go home for the operation, that she revokes the document on your allowance, giving it to you now, as you had been led to believe she would, and swears in writing that she won't interfere in your life again? It would have to be a legally binding document enforceable by law and that would take some time to draw up, I would imagine, so in the meantime she would have to go on dialysis. What do you think?'

'I think that sounds brilliant! I could probably spin out the legalities until after the exams are over and I'm sure the university would, if necessary, give me a leave of absence for such a serious thing.'

'Yes, I'm sure they would. The other advantage would be that you wouldn't have to feel guilty about not helping your mother in any way at all. You would have done your duty as a daughter.'

And there we left it, with me promising to keep in touch with her on everything that happened. I'm excited now about the phone call I'll be making home later.

***

Have just made the call but, as usual with my mother, it didn't turn out quite as I'd hoped. It went something like this:

Mother: Darling, is that really you? I knew you wouldn't desert your poor mother in her time of need.

Me: No, Mama. I'm not going to desert you but there are a couple of things you're going to have to do for me.

Mother (suspiciously): Oh, and what would they be?

And I told her of the conditions attached to my coming home.

Mother (screaming now): So it's blackmail now, is it? My own daughter is blackmailing me!

Me (as calmly as possible): If you want a kidney of mine, those are my terms. They are non-negotiable.

Mother slammed down the phone. But she rang back a while later. And this is how that conversation went:

Mother (wheedling): Darling, I'm sorry I was so angry before. Can't you just come home so we can discuss all this face-to-face?

Me: So you can get me into your slimy clutches again. No way!

Mother (angrily): You don't have to be rude, you know.

Me: I'm not being rude, just realistic.

Mother (sighing deeply): All right. We'll do it your way. But you'll have to come home to see my lawyer.

Me: No way again, Mama! Get him to send the papers up here. I've got my own lawyer, you know. (This wasn't true but I knew that I'd have to find one quickly.)

Mother (wailing now): But what am I going to do while this is all being sorted out?

Me (curtly): Go on dialysis like everyone else. Anyway, I'm sure if you pay the hospital enough, they can find you a suitable kidney quite quickly and then I won't have to come home at all. And if I do have the operation, it'll be up here, not at home. (I thought of these last two ideas on the spur of the moment.)

Mother (angry again): Oh, you heartless child!

This was the end of the conversation, which, frankly, left me very shaken. I knew my mother wasn't used to not getting her own way and I wondered what trouble I was storing up for myself by going against her wishes.

***

I've heard nothing from my dreadful mother for a couple of weeks now and I wonder if my blackmail (for, let's be honest, that's what it is) is working. In the meantime, I think I'll write a little about my love life up here.

I suppose the first thing to say about it is that it's been pretty turbulent. Needless to say, there's no shortage of boys here and I have availed myself of them freely but, unlike with my nameless waiter, always being careful and taking precautions. I didn't, however, go to bed with anyone from my own department as I felt that would be almost incestuous. But I soon got bored with students of my own age as they all seemed callow and, ultimately, boring to spend much time with. Also they showed me very little tenderness, unlike my humble waiter.

So I looked around for other ideas and one soon appeared in the shape of one of my lecturers, but from another department, who was younger than most of them and really rather good-looking. I had noticed him eyeing me in class and took the opportunity of meeting up with him for a personal tutorial. From there it was an easy job to seduce him and he did, indeed, prove a far more satisfactory lover than the young men I'd had thus far. He was married, however, which didn't bother me one bit, but did bother him and, although he said that he was prepared to leave his wife and elope with me, I never took this very seriously. And it turned out I was right not to, as one day he appeared and sobbed into my shoulder that he'd told his wife everything and that she was prepared to forgive him and take him back. So that was the end of that relationship.

I had more or less decided by then that all men were weak and ultimately heartless, only really being after one thing: sex, and as much of it as they could get. I knew, of course, that this was all driven by man's primitive brain, which told him in no uncertain terms to go forth and multiply, but I'd still expected a modicum of gentility in relationships to have developed over the centuries. So, yes, I did feel let down by my lecturer but I soon bounced back and vowed to live a celibate life and concentrate on my studies. And that is my position now: manless again and not caring much that I am. I get my sexual solace by masturbating myself to sleep and for the moment that seems to satisfy me. *(Good grief! Did I really write that? Well, I promised myself this would be as honest an account as I could make it.)*

I think I should finish here for now and get on with some work, but I'll be back, I promise, as soon as I have some real news to report.

Oh, yes. One final thing: I've found myself a lawyer, a woman who's prepared to help me check any documents I might receive. I hoped that a woman would be more sympathetic towards me than a man.

Chapter 6

Well, guess what! This morning in the post I got a large packet of documents, written in dense legalese, which *seemed* to be what I was waiting for. I skimmed them in amazement, thinking that my demented mama must be desperate for her new kidney and wondering how ill she really was. I rushed over to my lawyer's and dumped them all on her with instructions to take her time dealing with them, as I was still determined to at least finish my first year at uni, although there were only a few weeks left now. Then, if everything worked out, I could have the operation during the long summer vacation, which should give me enough time to recover, I hoped.

I rang Mama when I got back and told her that the papers were now with my lawyer who would be dealing with everything from now on and, strangely, for once she didn't have much to say. I wondered again how ill she was and asked her. She told me that the dialysis was a real pain and that she'd had to cut out all of her "little outings" – I quote. And could I PLEASE hurry up as she was getting desperate. Not once did she ask me how *I* was or whether I was enjoying my studies or, indeed, even *what* I was studying, but that's par for the course for her. She really is the most self-centred person I've ever met.

So now I can only wait to hear from my lawyer lady.

***

My lawyer got back to me the day before yesterday and told me that she'd finished work on the documents and they were ready for me to sign. She'd been in touch with my mother's lawyers, who had agreed after a certain amount of argumentation on a tightening up of some of the clauses in the contract and she said that she'd got me the best deal possible 'under the circumstances'. I pricked up my ears when I heard those last three words and said, 'Under what circumstances?' And then she seemed to become rather evasive, which really worried me. Could she have been bought out by my dear mama? Anyway, I said my thanks, adding it had taken less time than I'd expected, to which she replied that it hadn't been a particularly complex document.

This left me with a dilemma. Should I trust her or not? I knew about the power money had, even if I hadn't known much about the prices of things, and I was worried in case Mother had somehow put pressure on her. So I decided that I needed a second opinion and went back to my counsellor friend. We had another long chat, in which I brought her up to date with everything that had been going on, and, when I'd finished telling her the story and about my worries concerning the lawyer, she said at once, 'Follow your instincts, Annabelle. They seem to have served you well so far.'

I told her that my gut instinct was that I should no longer trust my solicitor and she said, 'Well, get yourself another one then.' It hadn't occurred to me that one could change lawyers like one could change doctors and I told her this. 'Of course you can,' she said. Then she added that, if it was her, she'd phone up my lawyer lady and ask her to post the documents back to me so that I could sign them in my own good time. This seemed extremely sensible to me and again I thanked her for her advice. I left her office feeling much happier and went back to my room where I promptly rang my solicitor and gave her the instructions we had decided on.

However, the phone call wasn't as straightforward as I'd thought it would be. The solicitor threw up all sorts of objections to posting the documents back to me, saying, for example, that I needed expert witnesses to watch me sign. I pointed out that there were hundreds of professional people at the university who would be prepared to help me with the signing. Then she seemed to become rather desperate and ended up almost pleading with me to come into her office and sign them there. This aroused my suspicions still further of her motives but I stuck to my guns, saying that I would only sign them under my own terms. Finally, she gave up and rather rudely agreed to post the completed documents back to me along with the bill for her services. She finished by saying, 'If you could bring them into my office duly signed and witnessed at your convenience, I would be most grateful.' And I told her I would. I hadn't mentioned my desire to show them to anybody else.

Then I knew I had to find myself another lawyer, an incorruptible one this time, and decided that I would have to go to the best in town. So, after looking through the Yellow Pages and writing down the names and addresses of a few that I thought might do, I jumped on my bike (Yes, that's how I get around now) and cycled into the city. The first couple I looked at did not seem to have the kind of premises I was looking for, but the third looked much more promising. It was in an old building right in the heart of the city and, when I went in, I was greeted by the familiar smell of money. Everything looked impressive, from the antique armchairs for waiting customers to sit in to the fine old paintings on the walls. This was surely the kind of place I needed.

I asked this time to speak to a senior partner of the firm and was told politely to wait. I wasn't asked why I needed to see someone at the top which pleased me too. My original lawyer had been a one-woman band without partners, and she had been working out of what, I saw now, were rather shabby premises. And therefore, I assumed, she was much more open to corruption.

I didn't have to wait long before an avuncular-looking older man, dressed immaculately in a sober suit with a blue shirt and tie and Italian loafers on his feet, came out of an office behind me and called my name. We introduced ourselves and he asked me to call him Peter, saying they didn't stand on formality in his company, which I liked. Then he asked what he could do for me. And I told him, without going into too many details of my background. He listened to me attentively and, when I'd finally stumbled to a halt, having told him the name of my probably former lawyer, he nodded his head and said, 'Yes, I think we can help you, Miss. As for your former solicitor, don't worry about her. If we find any anomalies in the contract, we will deal with her in our own time.'

'Thank you,' I said wholeheartedly. But then I added, 'Would it be possible for you to deal with this personally?'

He grinned at me and replied, 'I can see why you might be worried about some members of our revered profession. But yes, I don't see why not.'

And that's where we left it.

***

The documents arrived this morning by registered post, along with a massive bill for services rendered, and I rushed them over to my new lawyer. He was with a client when I arrived and I had to wait much longer this time to see him but he finally appeared and took me into his office. When I'd sat down, I passed him the package but, before he opened it, he said, 'I've done a bit of research on you and your mother and am satisfied that you are who you say you are.' That took me aback until I realised that he thought I might have been a fortune hunter.

'Good,' I said shortly.

Then he took out the documents and started to peruse them closely. After about fifteen minutes, he leaned back in his chair and said, 'Well, Annabelle, you were quite right to get a second opinion. If you'd signed up to what's in here, you'd have no guarantees of anything. You could drive a coach and horses through a lot of this.' And I breathed a huge sigh of relief. Then he said, 'I'm going to draw up a whole new watertight contract for you, which I will then show you before passing it on to your mother's lawyers. Is that okay with you?'

'Yes, that's fine,' I said.

'Ideally, you should have done it that way round in the first place but never mind about that now. It's not too late to start again. Oh, and, by the way, don't worry about this bill as it is, in fact, for services *not* rendered. We'll deal with it and, incidentally, our own services will be a lot cheaper than hers.'

'Thank you,' I gushed although, if everything went according to plan, I wasn't really worried about the money. I almost leant over his desk and kissed him.

I left, feeling that I was in good hands at last.

And he was as good as his word. I got a phone call from him, telling me that the contract was ready for me to view and the same afternoon, after lectures were over, I rushed again down to the city centre on my bike and went into the quiet splendour of the partnership. He met me and took me into his office, laying a much thinner document in front of me. 'Take as long as you like. You're welcome to annotate it. It's just a draft. I'll be around when you finish,' he said.

So I sat down and started reading. The first thing that struck me was the language. It was miles easier to read and understand than the contract sent to me by my mother's lawyers although it still had a number of legal words in it. But I think I understood it all and it was nearly exactly what I wanted. I added a few notes in the margins and sat back, pleased. Try and get out of that, witch! I thought happily to myself. Then I asked his secretary, who sat just outside, to call him back into his office which she did.

I asked him about the language first. Why was it written so differently from the other document which I'd had such trouble understanding? He laughed and said, 'Lawyers are supposed to be obfuscatory but it's not actually necessary most of the time. We believe that simple English is better for our clients and, therefore, better for us in the long run.' Another plus for his company, I thought.

Then we started talking about the contract itself and he reassured me on a few of my annotations, which were mainly about the meanings of some of the legal terminology, explaining clearly what was meant, and he added a few small points I'd suggested, writing everything down on his legal pad. It didn't take long and when we'd finished, he said, 'Come by tomorrow and you can pick up the final versions and sign them. I'll be the witness. Then all we have to do is post the copies off to your mother's solicitors and wait and see what happens. I would guess you're not too bothered either way.'

'No, you're right,' I said. 'If my mother refuses to sign, she doesn't get my kidney and I just continue on at university as normal. I'll manage fine without the money although it would be nice to know that she's never going to bother me again.'

And there we left it. I duly went back the following day, checked the contract and signed it and now I'm just waiting to hear from Mother.

***

I didn't have long to wait. I got a phone call from her about three days later. She seemed totally demented. She was screaming something about how I had let her down but it still wasn't too late. I put the phone on speaker and let her rant and rave while I was doing other things and finally she calmed down enough to ask in a more civilised tone, 'Are you there, Annabelle?' I said I was still there but it was impossible to talk to her while she was screaming at me. She had the grace to apologise but then went off again into another tirade. I finally got bored and just hung up.

She rang me back very quickly and said, 'How dare you hang up on me, child!' I pointed out that I was no longer a child but she didn't want to listen and started shouting again. Again I got bored and was about to hang up when she started crying. This disturbed me, as I'd never heard her cry before, even though I knew it was just another ploy.

I said, 'Oh, do stop the histrionics, Mama. They're not going to change anything. If you want one of my kidneys, why don't you just sign the bloody contract?' I knew I had to be firm with her otherwise she would just walk all over me, as she had done for so many years.

'How dare you go behind my back and employ a different solicitor!' she shouted now down the line, having miraculously, apparently, got over her tears.

'I'm just looking after my own interests,' I pointed out. 'I know you hate being thwarted but it's a simple enough document. If you don't want to sign, that's fine by me. I am perfectly capable of surviving by myself.'

She stopped then and considered my words. Then she said simply and calmly, 'Clearly you are grown up now and, as you say, perfectly capable of looking after yourself. In fact, I recognise in you some of the very qualities I had at your age. So, as the doctors have told me that it's very unlikely I'll find a match in the general population, I'll sign your wretched bit of paper.'

'Thank you, Mama. I'll wait to get my copy before I do anything about my kidney. Goodbye,' and I hung up, feeling rather pleased with my performance.

A couple of days later I got, via recorded delivery, the document back, duly signed by Mother. I took it over to Peter at once, who skim-read it and pronounced it perfectly satisfactory with no changes made. He said it might be better if he looked after the original in his safe and I agreed, so he made me a copy. My allowance was due to pay out in instalments every month, backdated to my eighteenth birthday, and he told me to keep a close eye on my bank account to make sure the money was going in, and I said I would.

Finally, he relaxed back in his chair and said, 'Well, I think that concludes our business, don't you? I suppose the next thing for you to do is to find out about the operation.'

'Yes,' I said, trying not to show my terror. Secretly I'd hoped that my mother wouldn't sign, as I've always had an irrational fear of hospitals. I'd never had to go inside one, having always been extremely healthy, and now I was committed to a major operation, which I was very scared of, although I knew it was done routinely these days. I said, 'Ideally, I would like to have it done up here at the beginning of the summer holidays.'

'I think that should be possible,' he said. 'Would you like me to do a bit of research to find out who the best man in the city is?'

'That would be very kind of you. I've got my exams coming up shortly and I don't think I can afford to spend any more time on this.'

'Okay. No problem,' he said.

Then, impulsively, I said, 'I'd like to take you out to dinner to celebrate. Would that be possible?' I'd noticed the wedding ring he wore and wasn't at all sure if his wife would approve or if it went against the ethics of his profession.

'I'd have to check with my partners but I don't see why not,' he replied.

'Great!' I said. 'Ring me when you know or have any news for me about the surgeon.' And he promised he would. Then I left.

Chapter 7

A couple of days later I got a call from him to say he'd okayed dinner with his partners and he'd found out about the surgeon. We agreed that the following Saturday night would be good for dinner and that he'd give me the information I'd asked for then. I asked him to choose a nice place for dinner and he said he knew the perfect place and gave me its name and address. 'I'll book a table,' he said.

'Fine,' I said and we hung up.

I knew I'd have to buy some more appropriate clothes than the tattered jeans, T-shirts and bomber jackets I wore around the university and decided to go on a shopping expedition into the city after classes were over.

Actually, I admit I rather enjoyed going out shopping for myself, and realised it was the first time I'd ever been able to buy some nice things with my own money. Always before I'd been accompanied by my wretched mother. I got a smart, black, sleeveless dress which seemed to show off my figure rather well and a pair of decent shoes. When I'd dressed up in them in my room, my friend, Emma, happened to come in to borrow something and caught me preening myself in front of my mirror.

'Wow! You look like a million dollars!' she exclaimed. 'Going somewhere fancy then?'

I told her about the date with my lawyer, adding, 'But don't worry. There'll be no hanky-panky. He's about a million years older than me and married.'

'That's never stopped you in the past, has it?' she said with a wicked grin. I told her to get lost and she left, giggling.

I knew I really had to catch up on my work and I settled down to it after changing back into my normal clothes and I actually managed to get quite a lot done over the next few hours.

The next few days passed uneventfully until Saturday came and I got dolled up for my dinner. I took a taxi to the restaurant which was a real luxury for me, but I didn't want to arrive on my bike, all sweaty and messed up. Once there I went down a long staircase into what must have been a large basement and came out into a dimly lit room with candles on the tables and linen tablecloths and napkins in place. Somebody was playing Gershwin quietly on a grand piano at the end of the restaurant. The atmosphere was lovely, very restrained, and I was pleased I'd made an effort with my appearance. I hadn't realised such places existed in the city.

Then I caught sight of my guest sitting at a table for two and he noticed me at the same time and waved. I went over to him, escorted by a waiter who pulled out my chair for me and presented me with a menu. 'I haven't been to a place like this since I left home,' I told Peter truthfully.

He was appraising me as I spoke and replied with the *non sequitur*, 'Well, you do look lovely tonight, my dear.' I blushed and said thank you. I noticed he was drinking mineral water and, as I wanted to keep my wits about me, I ordered a bottle too.

I had a look at the menu but then turned to the waiter and said, 'What do you recommend?' He pointed out a couple of dishes which sounded good and I ordered and Peter ordered the same.

Then, while we were waiting for the food to arrive, we did our business. I told Peter that the first tranche of money had been paid into my account and he told me the name of the man who, he assured me, was the most eminent kidney surgeon in the city and gave me his address and phone number, saying he was waiting for me to call. I thanked him and he asked if I was going to go private. I said I hadn't thought about it but, if it meant better treatment, then the answer was probably yes. And we left the topic there.

Our food arrived fairly quickly and we chatted a bit about our respective lives while we were eating. I found him a fascinating conversationalist and he seemed to have a real interest in me, not as a sex object but as a person, which was a bit of a novelty for me coming from a man. At one point he said, 'You're a remarkably mature young lady, you know, Annabelle,' and I blushed at the compliment.

I just replied, 'And you're a remarkably mature gentleman, Peter,' which made him laugh.

I asked him then how he'd discovered the restaurant and a kind of sadness came into his eyes. 'I used to bring my wife here when she was alive,' he said.

'Oh, so you're a widower,' I said, surprised.

'Yes,' he said shortly and I changed the subject for fear of offending him. We continued chatting about this and that and it seemed that the meal finished much too quickly.

'I have really enjoyed this evening, Peter,' I said truthfully.

He replied, 'So have I, Annabelle. So have I.'

After I'd paid with my credit card, he thanked me for the meal, saying 'It's very unusual for me to be taken out to dinner by a young lady, you know. It's usually me who takes people out and they're almost always much older than you.'

'Well, there's a first time for everything,' I said gaily and he grinned.

'How did you get here?' he said and I told him I'd come in a taxi. 'Let me take you home then. My car's just around the corner.' And I agreed. So he drove me back to my university accommodation and, on the way, I toyed with the idea of inviting him in but then decided against it, thinking what my housemates might say if they saw him.

Instead I asked, just before getting out of the car, 'Is there any chance of doing this again some time?'

'Yes, I'd like that,' he said. 'But it'll be on me next time.'

I'd undone my seatbelt by then and, impulsively, I know, I leaned over and kissed him on the cheek. Now it was his turn to blush. 'See you soon then,' I said and he waved goodbye.

That really was one of the best evenings of my entire life, I told myself happily as I bounced up to my room.

Chapter 8

Well, my end-of-year exams have come and gone and now I have no more excuses to postpone the operation. I've already been in touch with the surgeon, who had contacted my mother's doctors about her condition. Apparently, she was doing fine on the dialysis but was desperate to get my kidney so that she could resume her normal life again. He told me he could do the operation more or less when it suited me if I went private although it would take longer if I was to have it done on the NHS.

'How much would it cost if I had it done privately?' I asked and he mentioned a large sum but, as I mentioned, my allowance money had started to come through now. I'd had enough in reserve to pay Peter's bill and I felt it only right that I should pay for the operation as my original cash had come from my mother's gems. I knew it would leave me short but not for long. So I said yes to the private idea.

I suggested a date at the end of June to have it done and he said that would be fine. I asked how long the recuperation period would be and he replied that it depended on the individual but an average was about four to six weeks to get fully healed. Then I asked whether there would be any problems about getting my organ down to my mother and he said no, couriers ferried organs around the country all the time. It was all part of the service. When I got off the phone with him, I immediately rang my mother to tell her the date and she was pleased that I was going ahead with my side of the bargain, although I was still berated for taking so long. But I ignored her as I knew that very soon I'd be free of her for ever.

***

So today, with much trepidation, I went to a private hospital for preliminary tests and to sign all the relevant forms and actually I was quite surprised by the treatment I got. It was all very civilised, but personalised too, so that I was made to feel like a real human being, not just a statistic, and I wondered how similar it would have been had I had the operation done on the NHS. Everything was explained to me carefully and I signed all the relevant documentation, giving the surgeon permission to go ahead. Then I was sent home and told not to worry about a thing.

But that, of course, was impossible. I lay on my bed in the quiet house, thinking of the next morning when the operation was due to be carried out. They'd told me at the hospital that I would probably only need to stay there for a couple of days but, after that, I would need a few weeks' complete rest to make sure I'd healed up nicely. They'd asked me if I had anyone to look after me and I'd lied and said yes although, in fact, the house was empty now, all the students having left either to go on holiday or to go home. How I was going to manage I had no idea, but I felt sure that something or somebody would turn up to help me.

I thought of Peter and wondered if I could ring him and ask if he could pop round every other day or so and make sure I was still alive. However, I hadn't seen him since that first dinner and didn't want to bother him. I couldn't think of anybody else I could ask except – wait! What about the counsellor lady? She was a possibility. I'd kept her informed of everything that was going on and she did seem genuinely concerned about me. But I didn't know her private address or phone number and she wouldn't be around the university at present, it being holiday time. So I was stuck. At least I'd had the foresight to stock up the fridge. Oh, well. We will see.

***

As you know, I've been in hospital having one of my kidneys removed. At least I don't remember a thing about the operation itself as the anaesthetist had me knocked out cold. But what I do remember is waking up in the hospital bed, feeling very woozy with a throbbing pain in my stomach area. I looked under the bedclothes to see what I could, but the only thing visible was a mass of white bandages covering my stomach. I realised I was very thirsty but I didn't have the strength to call out to anybody. But then I remembered the red bell push they'd shown me to call a nurse if I needed one. I found it and pressed the button.

A nurse came in almost immediately and said, 'Oh, you're awake. That's good,' and started fussing around, taking my temperature and blood pressure. I croaked that I was thirsty and she gave me a long sip of water, which tasted better than any water I'd ever tasted before. Then, in a slightly stronger voice, I asked how the operation had gone.

'Everything went routinely as far as I'm aware,' she said. 'But you really need to speak to the surgeon who'll be coming in to see you shortly.'

I thanked her and she left. I'd forgotten to tell her about the pain. Damn! Oh well, I could live with it. So I just lay there waiting for the surgeon and wondering if this was how childbirth felt. Perhaps I'd get post-natal depression and I managed a grin at the thought.

He did, indeed, turn up quite soon and I at once asked him the same question I'd asked the nurse about how the operation had gone.

'No problems at all,' he said. 'Your kidney looked wonderful. Even as I speak it's winging its way down south to your mother. And I mean that literally. She sent a helicopter for it. As far as I know, it's the first time a private helicopter has landed here.' Yes, that would be typical of mother and I couldn't help smiling, even though it probably came out more like a wince. 'Are you in much pain?' he asked now.

'A bit,' I replied.

'I'll give you something for it,' he said and mentioned the name of a drug to a nurse who'd come in with him. 'Just try to take it easy, okay?' he said. 'You're clearly a tough cookie and should heal up very quickly.'

'Thank you, doctor,' I said, smiling up genuinely at him. It was the first time anyone had ever called me "a tough cookie" and I was thrilled. Then he left, promising to come back later in the day.

I was given the painkiller and it worked almost immediately. I was left feeling numb and fuzzy-headed but that was fine by me. The surgeon came back later after I'd managed to eat a little lunch and checked me over. He also changed my bandages so I could at last get a glimpse of what he'd done to me. But I was amazed to see almost no hole in my body even though I'd been told beforehand about the new endoscopic surgery, which meant it was unnecessary to leave large scars. I was pleased about that as I'd been worried in case my body ended up looking terribly deformed. He also said that they'd rapidly be decreasing the amount of painkillers I was getting, as they didn't want me to become addicted to them. He made this last point with a humorous grin and I knew he was only joking.

Then he left again and I lay back. You can imagine my surprise when, a couple of hours later, who should come through the door of my room but Peter. I was delighted to see him and asked how he'd known when I was going to be operated on. He smiled and said, 'I asked the surgeon to keep me informed.'

'Well, I'm jolly glad he did,' I replied.

'How are you feeling?'

'Okay, I guess. I've missed you.'

'It's always nice to be missed,' he said with a mischievous grin. Then he continued more seriously, 'I've actually come to ask if maybe you'd like to recuperate at my house. I have a lovely housekeeper who's always looked after me when I've been poorly, and I know she'd be delighted to do the same for you. I know your student house is empty now and I just thought it might be more convenient for you.'

'Oh, Peter. That would be fantastic! I've been a bit worried about how I was going to cope by myself. But how did you know the house was empty?'

'I've been keeping an eye on you from afar,' he said with a twinkle in his eye.

'Do you mean spying on me?'

He held up his hands in mock horror and said, 'Heaven forfend! No, not at all. Just looking out for your best interests.'

'Oh, well, that's all right then, I guess,' I said, rather ungratefully I know.

'Anyway, I hear everything went well.'

'Yes, it seems to have done. The surgeon called me a tough cookie.'

'There's a compliment if ever I heard one.'

And so the banter went on. Finally, when we seemed to have run out of words, I said, 'Don't you have work to do?'

'Actually, no. I've had some holiday due to me for a while and I've decided to take it now.' I wondered if the timing was anything to do with me but didn't push the point. I was much too grateful to him. But then he said, 'I do have a few things to do, however. So I'll come by when you're due to be released and take you over to your house so you can collect what you need. Okay?'

I was feeling overwhelmed by all this kindness and just said, 'That would be great. Thanks ever so much, Peter.'

***

And that is why I am writing this in Peter's beautiful old farmhouse out in the countryside. It's now a couple of weeks after the operation and I'm feeling more or less one hundred percent already. I'm so pleased with the way everything went and so grateful to Peter for putting me up. What he said about having a lovely housekeeper turned out to absolutely true. She's called Mary and originally came from Ireland. She's one of the most delightful people I've ever met and has looked after me as if I were her own daughter.

While I've been here, I have had the chance to find out more about Peter and his dead wife and have looked at all the photos of her around the house. According to Peter, she was a lawyer like himself and they met during their studies and fell in love at once, getting married soon after at a young age. They'd never managed to have any children, however, which was a bitter blow to them both, and she died of cancer a few years ago. That's it in summary. What a romantic and tragic story, I thought to myself after I'd heard it. I was grateful to Peter yet again for sharing it with me.

As I'm almost better now and Peter had reached the end of his holiday, I decided it was time to go back to my student house. So I said a tearful goodbye to both of them, saying, absolutely truthfully, 'I wish I'd had proper parents like you two,' and got a warm embrace from Mary. I had to promise her to come and see them as often as possible, which was an easy promise to make and, I hope, to keep.

***

Guess what? I've found a job! What about that?! It's my first ever and I'm determined to do it to the best of my ability. I know it's only in a bar serving drinks, but at least it's a real job and I'm at last earning my own money. It means a lot of late nights but I don't mind that as I can always sleep in the next day. However, the new term will be starting again soon and I also want to get ahead, if I can, with my work, so I'm doing some reading in the mornings. Peter has dropped in occasionally, I guess to check up on me, and I've been back to his house once on my day off. Still no men or even handsome boys on the horizon though, but again I don't mind. Perhaps I could become a nun when I finished uni? An idea which made me smile inwardly. I've given no thought at all to what I would do after I finished my studies but it all seemed so far away.

I've heard nothing at all from my mother, which suits me fine, and I presume the operation has gone okay for her too. Hopefully, she is now out of my life forever.

Chapter 9

Nothing much has happened over about the past eighteen months until very recently. My studies have been progressing well and I've continued working during the holidays in the bar. Actually, I've rather enjoyed that, especially being able sometimes to have a chat with the regulars when it's not too busy. The manager told me the other day that he was thinking of promoting me as I'd done so well but I know I don't want to work behind the scenes. Of course the money isn't important for me, as my allowance is being paid regularly into my account, and I know I am now quite a wealthy young woman. It is reassuring to know that I'll be able to leave uni without any debts, unlike most of my contemporaries. It's the getting out and meeting new people which is the key thing. I am already much more confident around "normal" people and that's important to me. I feel now that I could hold my own in the "real" world.

However, the other day another bombshell concerning my mother fell from the skies. I got a phone call from her lawyer saying that she'd had a stroke and was asking for me. Was she actually dying? I couldn't imagine that. I didn't know what to do and asked Peter.

'Ring them up first and ask how bad she is,' was his advice and I took it. When I rang back, the lawyer said that she was very weak and helpless, paralysed down one side of her body, and needed twenty-four/seven professional care.

'What's the prognosis?' I asked.

'It doesn't look good,' he said. Then he said something which really took me aback. 'If she dies, you do realise that you're her only heir, don't you?'

Me in charge of all that money? I couldn't imagine that. 'How badly does she want to see me?' I asked.

'All I can tell you is that she's made a new will with you as the only beneficiary and, every time I've been to the house, she asks when you're coming. The last time I went, she said, "I don't think I've got long. Please can you tell Annabelle to come and see me? I really need to talk to her."'

That left me in a real quandary. The last thing in the world I wanted was to go home but, after our huge row, why had she now left me all her money? Had she had a change of heart about me? Did she want to apologise to me? I rang Peter and told him about the conversation I'd had with the lawyer and he said that what I did was up to me of course, but he reckoned that my mother could do me no more harm and, if she really was dying, then he thought it would be right of me to go and see her.

I thought long and hard about what he'd said and finally decided that it wouldn't hurt to make a quick trip down south, although I wouldn't stay in my old home. I'd find a hotel nearby. And I'd keep the visit as short as possible. The decision made, I rang the lawyer and told him I'd be down the following weekend.

And that's where we are now. More when I come back.

***

Have just got back from the south and what a story I have to tell you!

I booked into a hotel not far from home and, after resting up overnight, I rang the lawyer, whose name was David, the next morning. He said he'd be round to pick me up and take me to see my mother in an hour or so. I put on a pretty frock I'd bought for myself and a little of my own jewellery and generally made myself look presentable. David already knew that it was one of my conditions of seeing my mother that he'd be there too. I had no intention of walking into the lion's den alone.

He turned up on time and we drove home, my trepidation growing all the time. However, when we got there, we couldn't see Mother immediately as she was having some physiotherapy done. So we hung about in one of the drawing rooms until we were summoned. We went on up to her bedroom and, when I walked in, I literally didn't recognise the creature I saw lying in her bed. She looked like an old wizened crone and I suddenly felt a pang of sympathy for her. That was a shock in itself and I wondered where it had come from.

Then in a very weak, frail voice my mother summoned me to her and I sat next to her bed on a chair which had already been put there. There were four people in the room as, apart from my mother, myself and David, there was also a nurse keeping a watchful eye on her. She'd told me as I went in that I shouldn't tire her or get her excited and I said I'd do my best.

'I'd like to give you a hug,' my mother began, 'but, unfortunately, it's not possible as my left hand isn't working.' I looked down at it and it appeared to be now more like a claw than a hand. She continued, 'Thank you for coming, darling. I wasn't at all sure if you would. Fortunately, I still have my wits about me but I don't know how long that's going to last.' Here she paused and seemed to struggle for breath. But after a few seconds she carried on, 'I needed you to come because I wanted to say how sorry I am for trying to control your life and not being around much while you were young. I realise now that I was wrong and I'm very pleased with the way you've turned out. You obviously have great strength of character.' And there she stopped. You could have knocked me over with a feather when I heard these words and I felt tears welling up inside me but I pushed them back.

Then she picked up steam again and said, 'The other reason I needed to see you is a legal one. David has drawn up some documents and I would be most grateful if you would sign them.' Not more documents, I groaned inwardly. She must have caught the expression on my face because she added at once, 'Don't worry, child. There's nothing bad in them.' And then she lay back on her bed with, I saw now, a sheen of sweat on her face. 'Goodbye, Annabelle, probably for the last time.' Were those tears I saw glittering in the corners of her eyes? I couldn't be sure.

I hadn't said a single word during all this but now I felt impelled to do or say something. So I just leant over her and gave her a kiss on the cheek and she looked up at me with astonishment (and was it delight?) written all over her face. But the nurse now intervened, saying, 'That's quite enough for now. I think it's time for the two of you to leave.' So we did.

I didn't know what to say to David as he drove me back to the hotel. Was it really possible to change one's character so completely? Even on one's death bed? But finally I said, 'What are these documents she wants me to sign?'

'They give you and me lasting power of attorney over her affairs if she should become incapable of making decisions by herself,' he said.

'Oh,' I replied, shocked once more into disbelieving silence. But then I said, 'Does she really trust me enough to do that?'

'I think the answer is clear,' he said. 'Yes, she does. And she trusts you enough to take over her entire fortune when she dies.'

'But I neither want nor need any more money!' I wailed.

'Nevertheless, it will be yours to do with as you wish.'

That shut me up and when we got back to the hotel, we went into the lounge area and sat down at a small table. He took from his briefcase a wodge of papers and I read them through with more understanding now than I'd had at the beginning of this whole saga. They seemed to be in order and I asked just one question. 'Am I right in thinking that we both need to sign if Mother needs anything, should she become incapable of making her own decisions?'

'Yes,' he replied simply.

'Okay,' I said and signed the papers where he showed me. He then signed them himself below Mother's scrawly signature.

'Well,' he said, 'I think that concludes our business today, Annabelle. I would just like to thank you on behalf of your mother for making the journey down here and to apologise myself for attempting to subvert the original contract. But you do understand, I hope, that I only did it on your mother's orders. Oh, and one final thing on a personal note: I'm glad that you seem to have made up with your mother, even if it is at the end of her life.'

'So am I,' I replied. And he left. I went on up to my room, threw myself on the bed and wept bitter tears of regret now for everything that had happened between Mother and myself, for all the might-have-beens.

The next day I went back up to uni in a thoughtful frame of mind. I knew I wasn't ready to assume the vast responsibility of managing my mother's fortune but didn't know what to do about it. So, as usual, I rang Peter and told him what had transpired down south. And, as usual, he gave me good advice. He said I should first finish my degree and then possibly think about doing a business course, which would give me a thorough grounding in all aspects of the business world. I thought that sounded like an excellent idea and I thanked him.

By the way, I have said almost nothing about my studies. If you remember, my original reason for studying psychology was to try to get some sort of insight into my mother and myself. But I actually found the whole field fascinating even though it hadn't really helped me with her. I thoroughly enjoyed all the lectures and even writing the essays, especially the research I had to do for them. My lecturers were all pleasant, informative and supportive. So I was very happy with my choice of subject and had been predicted a good degree at the end of my studies. I really wanted to go into the field of psychology, possibly doing research later, but I knew with heart-sinking certainty that this ambition would probably be impossible to fulfil if I had to manage my mother's money. Was she even going to reach out to me beyond the grave? Would *that* be her final revenge?

I knew also that it would be irresponsible to simply give all the money away, as I had once wanted to. It would be better to use it for good but on what? I had simply no idea at present. But of course all this worrying was way off in the future some time. I firmly believed my mother to be indestructible, in spite of how she'd seemed when I saw her. Anyway, I had to get on and finish my degree first.

Chapter 10

About four months have now passed and everything was going fine until I had another phone call from David a few days ago. He said that Mother had just died peacefully in her sleep from another massive stroke and her funeral would take place the following weekend in the city cathedral. He asked me if I would be going but the news was such a shock that I didn't answer him but just hung up. So my prediction about her immortality hadn't come true – worse luck! I was just coming up to my finals and was inundated with revision. But I knew I had to go. How did I feel? Conflicting emotions is the answer. On the one hand, I felt sad, but no sadder than if anyone else I knew had passed away, and on the other, I felt what I thought was relief. I didn't cry, if that's what you want to know. Not at first anyway.

After a while thinking these things, I knew I had to ring David back and say yes, I'd be there. So I did that and he seemed pleased. He asked if I wanted to stay in the big house or in the hotel nearby. I told him the hotel again, as I couldn't stand the thought of being in the house where I'd been so unhappy for so long. After that I rang Peter and told him the news and about my imminent return south for the funeral. So on Friday morning I packed a bag and took a taxi to the train station. As before, the journey seemed endless but I had plenty of work to occupy me and finally I reached the hotel, where I had a hot bath and a decent dinner before I went to bed. Against my expectations, I slept well and got up the next morning feeling refreshed.

I'd bought myself a severe black trouser suit for the occasion and put it on, putting my long hair up as well. Looking at myself in the mirror, I reckoned I looked demure enough for a funeral. I'd arranged to meet David in a bar in the city centre, just a stone's throw from the cathedral, and after a late breakfast I took a taxi there. As I got in, I thought that I was probably now rich beyond my wildest dreams and could take taxis whenever I wanted.

It was still early and the bar was empty. 'Do you want a drink?' David asked when he came in just after me.

'No, thanks,' I replied. 'Just some water.'

He got my water and brought over something that looked like a gin and tonic for himself. 'Well, Annabelle,' he said. 'It's good to see you looking so well. We have a lot to discuss.'

'I guessed you'd say something like that,' I replied. 'But please don't ask me to sign anything today.'

'Of course not. But I was wondering what plans you'd made for the future now that you'll inherit everything. I know you want to finish your degree first but that's not far away now, is it?' I shook my head and he continued. 'I was wondering specifically what you want to do with the house and its contents. I think that should be an immediate priority, don't you?'

I nodded in agreement but then said, 'Sorry, David, but I haven't given it any thought. Don't you think that we should wait until my mother's been buried before we decide what to do with her things?'

He had the grace to blush and said quickly, 'Yes, of course. I'm sorry if I offended you.' Then he added, 'It's just that I've been trained to think practically.' He looked at his watch and said now, 'It's probably time for us to be getting over to the cathedral. Were you aware that your mother had planned her funeral down to the last detail?'

'No, I wasn't. But it doesn't surprise me in the least.'

'Yes, it's going to be quite a fancy do. Everybody important in the city has been invited and the bishop's going to deliver the eulogy.'

'Just as long as I don't have to say anything,' I said grimly.

'No, you won't have to say or do anything except for being at the front of the receiving line after the service to thank everybody for coming. They'll all want to offer you their condolences. Oh, and, of course, appear at the burial afterwards and, if you want to, at the wake. It's to be held in the house. But that is very much optional.'

'Okay, I can probably handle all that,' I said grimly again.

'Good. Let's go then, shall we?' And he led me out of the bar and across the big square to the doors of the cathedral. I hadn't visited it for many years although I'd been inside a few times when I was on school trips, and I was amazed by its sheer scale. Yes, I thought bitterly. This would be the only place Mother would have liked to be seen off from. But I said nothing and followed David down to the front, my head held high. The cathedral seemed to be almost full but there were two empty places in the front row of pews and we sat down. I wondered how many of the people there were true friends of Mother's and how many were there just to show their faces. I'd never known Mother to have real friends who she could just chat with about normal things, just advisors, like David, and hangers-on.

Then the great organ started up and everybody stood and sang a hymn that I thought I recognised but I didn't sing along. I just stood there looking around curiously at the sea of faces around me. I spotted a man sitting near the front with a big gold chain around his neck and reckoned he must be the mayor, but I couldn't have put a name to anyone. I did, however, recognise a few of the people who'd used to hang out with Mother at home.

The closed coffin was already lying at the front near the altar and after the hymn the bishop appeared and started talking about Mother, especially the things she had done for the city and her patronage of the arts. But then his tone changed and he started to become more personal, listing all Mother's qualities. I didn't recognise her at all from his description and almost burst out laughing, especially when he said what a wonderful mother she'd been to me. He finally finished talking and after a certain amount of religious mumbo-jumbo, such as sprinkling the coffin with holy water, he left the stage and stood on one side while everybody sang a couple more hymns. Then Mother's coffin was carried outside by four burly men, I presumed to the hearse which must be waiting outside, prior to the burial.

And that was about it. The service hadn't lasted as long as I'd feared. David and I stood up and walked back to the main doors while everybody filed out, giving me their condolences as David had said they would. I felt them all looking curiously at me, wondering probably if I would continue my mother's policies with her money. The bishop came out last, took both my hands in his and said how terribly sorry he was for my loss and how heart-broken I must be, but I just inclined my head a little at his words, murmuring a thank you as I had done with everybody else. I hadn't felt like crying at all during the whole thing. It didn't seem real to me; it was as if I was watching a play.

Then we got into the Rolls, which was waiting outside, and set off for the cemetery, following the hearse and being followed by a long stream of other cars. It wasn't far away and inside I noticed at once the large new tombstone Mother must have had erected in the past few months. It was like burying a Pharaoh, I thought, and I wondered idly whether any horses, or indeed humans, were also being buried alongside her to help her into the afterlife, but then I chastised myself for my levity. It was a lovely, sunny day and I wondered also whether Mother had engineered it that way, a cause for more self-chastisement.

The coffin was lowered into the open grave and David whispered to me to go forward and throw the first handful of earth onto it. I didn't really want to do this but went as instructed and picked up a handful from the big pile standing beside the grave. After that I went up to the hole in the ground and looked down at the coffin.

But then I was amazed to find myself crying. I had no idea where the tears came from and I was shocked by them. However, at that moment I knew I was free of my mother at last and I threw the earth almost angrily into the hole and walked back to where David was standing, the tears streaking my make-up. David put his arm around my shoulder but I just kept on crying. The tears wouldn't stop and I felt very embarrassed by them. But there was nothing I could do and I just let them flow. Finally, however, they did dry up and I knew they had been cathartic in some sense.

The funeral finished and I told David to give my apologies to everybody at the wake but that I really didn't think I could handle it. He was very sympathetic and just drove me back to my hotel in silence. I felt shattered and just went back to my room and lay on the bed. I fell asleep but it was a disturbed sleep, disturbed not only by my strange feeling of loss but also by a number of weird dreams which I couldn't quite remember when I woke up. But I felt fine again afterwards and somehow I knew that those would be the last tears I would ever shed for my mother.

I started thinking about what else I had to do and remembered David asking me what I wanted to do about the house. I pondered the question as I lay on my bed and decided I was determined to sell it as it held too many unhappy memories for me. I would auction off any valuables inside like my mother's jewels and art collection, and ask that everything else be donated to charity shops. Then I remembered the staff. What on earth would I do with them? I couldn't just throw them out on the streets. Many of them had been with my mother for years and some since before I was born. I decided that I would offer them all a generous settlement, depending on their length of service, which could come out of the profits from the house. That decision made, I felt much happier and knew I could go back to uni with a clear conscience. I'd ask Peter to draft David a formal letter when I got back, detailing my decision, and leave it all up to him to execute.

I felt hungry then, as I'd missed lunch, so I went to the dining room and had a proper dinner with a few glasses of wine. Feeling full and a little tipsy afterwards, I went back up to my room and, after a long hot shower, fell asleep again and this time I slept normally.

On the way back to uni the following day I started thinking about the responsibilities the money would bring and what I could do with it. I had no idea how much I was worth and didn't care but, if it really was a lot, I knew I had a duty to spend it wisely. Fortunately, nobody at the university except the counsellor knew that I was an heiress and I intended to keep it that way. Nobody knew anything either about the circumstances of my birth and I hoped that information had died with Mother.

Then I had what I thought was a good idea. I would set up full scholarships for two bright but poor people who wanted to study at my university, one for a home student and one for an overseas student. But I wanted to keep it quiet. I didn't want my name being trumpeted from the rooftops, which would just be embarrassing. Also I had to bear in mind that I would be a target for fortune hunters and I was determined to resist that by any means possible. Another question then to ask Peter's advice about: how to achieve all that? Suddenly, however, a different thought occurred to me: What if I never found a lifelong partner like my mother hadn't? Wouldn't that be sad?! But I'd cross that bridge when I came to it. I certainly didn't want to get married yet.

So with all these thoughts mulling about in my head, I got back to uni and my regular existence. I spoke to Peter as soon as I returned and he promised to write a formal letter to David, laying out my wishes for the house, saying that of course he would show it to me before he sent it. He said he would have to do some research on the scholarship idea and especially on how to keep my name out of it. I told him that he wasn't to do all this out of affection for me. I would certainly pay him whatever he felt was right and he laughed and said, 'Don't be silly. Now I know you can afford it, I'll be sending you a whopping bill.' And once more I knew how lucky I was to have found a friend in him.

One other thing happened at this time. David sent me a news cutting from the local paper down south with a picture of me crying at my mother's graveside and a headline which screamed "Local Heiress Cries at Mother's Funeral", followed by a longish article reiterating all the points the bishop had made about everything she'd done for the city. He'd included a note which said, 'I hope the journalists don't find you up north but I fear they will.'

Chapter 11

Well, my finals are at last over! I haven't got the results yet but I think I did reasonably well. I asked David not to get in touch with me in the period between the funeral and finals as I didn't want to be distracted. And he's not done so. But now I know I have to head back into the real world and see to my mother's estate. I presume it's been ticking over okay and hasn't been looted by anyone. It's the last thing in the world I actually want to do, but I can't evade my responsibilities any longer.

So I rang Peter and asked him what I needed to know from Mother's advisors. He suggested setting up a meeting with them all, especially her accountants, and said that, if I wanted, he could attend. I thought that was a great idea and thanked him yet again. 'Don't thank me until after you get my bill,' he said jokingly. So I rang David and asked him for a date for the meeting and he said he'd get back to me, which he's just done, setting the date nearly a week from now.

I thought I'd just mention my love life, which, if you remember, was pretty barren by the end of my first year at uni. Believe it or not, but I've only had one fling since then with a good-looking PhD student. I thought I was in love with him for a while until I got bored with his conversation. Almost the only thing he could talk about was his thesis and, as he was an engineer, I understood very little of what he was saying. So that's been it since then and I haven't really missed men at all.

After that I flirted with lesbianism for a short while and had a fling with one of my housemates but didn't enjoy it much and soon dropped the whole experiment; fortunately, I managed to stay friends with the girl afterwards. At least, however, I now knew I was thoroughly hetero in my sexual orientation.

I realise I haven't said anything about drugs as an undergraduate. The reason for this is simple: they didn't actually play much part in my life at that time, unlike for many of my contemporaries. I quickly got to know my limits with cannabis (a couple of drags from a spliff) and never went on to anything harder. I suspect this was because I hated the feeling of losing control. It was the same with alcohol for me back then, so I guess I just don't have an addictive personality.

Chapter 12

Just got back from the meeting and how interesting it was! We met in a conference centre and sat around a huge table with myself and Peter on one side and an array of dark suits on the other. The only one I recognised was David, who was dressed surprisingly casually in a nice suit but without a tie. I was introduced to them all but promptly forgot their names. They could have been interchangeable robots as far as their looks went.

Then we got down to business. I allowed Peter to speak for me and he started by asking for a list of Mother's assets which one of the accountants produced. It was a very long list and I skimmed it quickly. It seemed as if Mother had had her fingers in an awful lot of pies and I asked what the total value was.

The accountant hesitated for a moment but then said, 'Somewhere in the region of 364 million pounds after inheritance tax.' I gasped and collapsed back into my chair. So I really was an heiress! But I swiftly recovered and Peter asked a lot more very specific questions, taking notes of the answers on his legal pad. I took very little part in that bit of the meeting as I was thinking of the good I could perhaps do with such an enormous fortune.

When we broke for coffee, I went up to David and asked him what was happening with the house and he told me it was up for sale and there had been a number of bids. He was just waiting a little longer to see if anybody went higher. Also the staff had been told and all of them had seemed satisfied with the settlement I'd proposed. Then I told him about my plan to set up the two scholarships at my university, which I hadn't mentioned to him yet, and he nodded approvingly at my idea. I said that I was still waiting for the results of Peter's research on how to do the whole thing quietly and he nodded again, seeming to understand my reasons for wanting to do it that way. He said that, once I gave the go-ahead, the money would be forthcoming immediately, and I thanked him.

'What are you intending to do with the rest of the money?' he asked and I told him I hadn't decided yet. Then he said, 'You are going to need full-time advisors, you know,' and I told him I was well aware of that although I hadn't decided who yet. I mentioned Peter's idea of my doing a business course so that I wouldn't be quite so lost when it came to the money and he nodded again, saying, 'Yes, I think that's a very wise move. Your mother seemed to do everything by instinct and, although it usually worked, she did make some horrendous mistakes.'

'What about her patronage of the arts in the city?' I asked now. 'I'm not actually very interested in continuing that but, if you recommend I do, I will certainly consider it. But please remember that I won't be able to go to any of the appalling galas that Mother used to so love attending.'

'I quite understand,' he said soothingly. 'And you won't have to if you don't want to. But I would suggest keeping up with the relatively small amounts she paid the various institutions in the city every year. It's good public relations apart from anything else.'

'Okay,' I said, 'that sounds sensible.'

So all that having been discussed, we went back into the meeting. Since Peter seemed happy with the replies he'd been given and had nothing else to ask, he laid the floor open to anyone who wanted to say something. And many of the suits did. They all had suggestions on ways to improve Mother's business, usually connected with selling off some of the assets which weren't profitable and investing the money elsewhere, and Peter took careful notes of all of them while I just listened and learned. It was like a crash course in business and I picked up quite a bit of useful information.

What struck me most was the amazing diversity of Mother's business affairs from controlling shares in a nickel mine in Canada to part ownership of a shipping company to many different kinds of manufacturing companies. I asked at one point how many of the assets mentioned were things she'd inherited from her father and how many were things she'd initiated herself and was surprised by the answer. It seemed that more than half were businesses she'd got into herself after her father died. I hadn't realised quite what an astute business brain she must have had.

The meeting finally ended with no firm decisions made as I said I needed time to think about everything before I changed any of my mother's ideas and David took Peter and me out to lunch. When we'd ordered, I said, 'Well, it's certainly given me a lot to think about.'

David grinned and said, 'Yes, I'm not surprised. You've really been thrown in the deep end, haven't you?' Then he added, 'Have you thought at all about what you're going to do when the tabloids catch up with you? After all, it's not every day that a young, attractive heiress comes along.'

I shuddered and said, 'Don't! I guess I'll just have to cross that bridge when I come to it.'

Peter then broke in and said, 'I think David's got a point. You do need to decide how you're going to evade reporters.'

'Well, I'm not locking myself away in a big house in the country, only appearing for fancy do's with my so-called peers like my mother did. I'll tell you that for nothing!' I said angrily.

'Okay, Annabelle, okay,' David said soothingly. 'We're not asking you to do that but you will need to give some thought to the problem if you're not to be pestered for the rest of your life.'

'Yes, I know, I know,' I almost wailed.

Then our food came and we dropped the subject and ate in silence. After lunch we said goodbye to David and, armed with the files we'd been given, we took the train back up north. Peter spent most of the journey typing up his notes onto his laptop while I perused the files, occasionally asking questions if there was anything I didn't understand. We were nearly there when I remembered something David had said about advisors. I asked Peter where he thought I might find people with the right sort of background who I could trust implicitly to do the right thing for me and my fortune.

He looked askance at me when I asked and said, 'Sorry. I really can't help you with that. But it might be a good idea to keep on a few of your mother's old advisors, don't you think? At least they know her business.' He added, 'Of course I will help you in any way I can.'

'I knew you would say that but I feel you've devoted quite enough time to me recently. Isn't it about time you went back to your proper job?'

He laughed and said, 'This is part of my "proper job" as you put it. Don't forget you're paying me to help you.'

'Yes, but...' and I floundered to think what to say. I knew he would not be doing as much for me if he hadn't felt in some way responsible for me. I realised suddenly he'd become like a father figure to me, something, of course, I'd never had before.

'No buts,' he said. 'Just be grateful you've got an impartial observer on your side. Where are you going to live now, by the way? Are you going to stay on in the student house? Can you indeed do that?'

'Too many questions,' I cried. 'I don't know the answers yet. I suppose it depends on my acceptance onto the postgraduate business course I've applied for at the university. If they say yes to me, I don't see why I couldn't stay on there, for a while at least. But I think it's unlikely they will since I have no experience of business and not even a first business degree.'

'Don't forget what we said about the tabloids catching up with you. It might be unfair to your housemates if *they* got pestered by reporters.'

I hadn't thought of that. 'I suppose it might be better to rent a flat somewhere,' I said hesitantly.

'You could buy one if you wanted,' Peter pointed out. 'Property's always a good investment.'

'I need to make a proper list of everything I've got to do,' I said.

And then we arrived at our station and got off the train. I said goodbye to Peter and he promised to get a readable summary of everything that had been said at the meeting to me in the next few days. I thanked him and gave him a peck on the cheek. Then I headed off to my house and I have been typing this up for the past few hours. I wanted to do it immediately so that I wouldn't forget anything. And now I think I'm in a position to make that list but not till tomorrow. I'm tired and am going to bed.

***

Well, guess what? I've got my results and I got a first! I am delighted with this news as it has confirmed for me something I've always felt unsure about: I have a brain! My dear departed mother never once suggested to me I might be clever and consequently, I have never thought of myself as such. After all, she'd put me down to do a course at a finishing school, which requires, as far as I know, no brains at all!

And then, hard on the heels of this, came another bit of good news. I've been accepted onto the business course. I wonder who put in a good word for me. Was it Peter, or perhaps one of my psychology professors? Anyway, it means I can stay on in my adopted city for another year, but it's made the issues about Mother's fortune more pressing. Luckily, I have the whole of the summer holiday ahead of me to sort everything out.

Do you remember the list of things I had to do? Well, here it is, exactly as I first wrote it down, minus one point about checking with the business department about the status of my application, which no longer applies:

> 1) Find out from Peter re my scholarship idea. How soon can it be set up and how much will it cost?
> 2) Go south again and interview Mother's old advisors with a view to hiring someone to help me with the business. Take somebody with me?
> 3) Check out flats in the city.
> 4) Learn to drive!

I haven't mentioned the last point before, but I know it will be important for me in the future. I certainly don't want to be ferried around by chauffeurs for the rest of my life like Mother had been.

Anyway, I started by ringing Peter and telling him the good news. He was delighted for me and congratulated me warmly. I asked him whether he'd had a hand in getting me accepted into the business department and he replied enigmatically, 'Why ever would I want to do a thing like that? I'm sure it was the strength of your application that got you accepted.'

I didn't push him on the point, but asked instead, 'What's going on with my scholarship idea?'

'I think we're nearly there,' he told me. 'I've spoken to the relevant people at the university and they say that anonymous bequests are not that uncommon. It would be in the form of a trust fund and I have already started drafting the documents for that. The fund would give to worthy recipients the money for tuition, books and accommodation plus a smallish amount of spending money, enough for the applicants' basic needs. This has all been done before so it doesn't entail much work for me. The fund would need to be self-sustaining from the interest it would generate if it's going to last for ever and such a fund would cost somewhere in the region of £500,000 for two scholarships. I hope that answers all your questions, Annabelle.

Are you sure you wish to proceed with it? I have to ask that, you know.'

'Yes, absolutely sure, thanks, Peter.'

'Okay. It should be ready to start by this time next year.'

'Oh,' I said, disappointed. 'I was hoping it could start this autumn term.'

'I'm afraid not, Annabelle. The university has only recently been told about it and they need to choose the two best applicants first. That takes time and the physical setting up of the scholarships takes time too. There are quite a lot of steps to go through before the university will be satisfied that everything is kosher. But there is no doubt that they are very grateful to you. They told me to pass on their warmest thanks to my client.'

'Okay,' I said. 'I understand.' Then I said, 'There is another point you might be able to help me with, Peter. As I mentioned to you, I've got to appoint somebody to look after my business interests, especially over the next year when I'll be studying, and have decided that the best way to do it is to take your advice and return south to interview as many of my mother's old advisors as I can, with a view to choosing the most suitable person, or people, to help me. But I don't have the confidence or knowledge to do this by myself. I was wondering if you could spare somebody from your firm to help me out.

Possibly somebody who has experience of interviewing?'

There was a pause while Peter thought about it and then he said, 'Yes, I don't see why not. I know the very person to help you. She's on our human resources team and has plenty of experience interviewing. And you'd be able to trust her absolutely. How long do you think you'd need her for?'

'A couple of days at most, I would think,' I said.

'Okay. I'll ask her.'

'Thanks ever so much, Peter, as always. You really are a gem.' And there we ended the conversation. Then I rang David and told him of my plan to come south for the interviewing and asked if he could get as many of Mother's old advisors as he could to send me their CVs and letters of application for the post of Managing Director in my absence. I added, 'You can tell them that the remuneration for their services, if they're appointed, will be substantial if that helps.'

He promised he'd do that very soon and we both hung up. Another thing taken care of, I thought wryly.

Chapter 13

But then, a few days later, the disaster I'd been fearing above all others and which both Peter and Graham had warned me about, occurred. I'd been doing some chores around the house and decided to go for a bike ride to clear my head. So I went as usual down the stairs to collect my bike which was standing in the hall. However, through the stained glass panes of the front door I suddenly noticed a scrum of people waiting patiently, it seemed, just outside the gate to the front garden and I wondered what was going on. I stepped outside and was immediately bombarded by flash-lights going off and people shouting at me. They were asking questions like, 'How much are you worth, Miss?' and 'What are you going to do with your new fortune?' I was completely taken by surprise and didn't know what to say or do. I just stood there at the entrance with my mouth open. Then I whirled round and ran back inside, slamming the door behind me.

So they'd found me! I wondered how for a moment, but then realised it didn't matter. But then I wondered what rubbish about me would be printed in tomorrow's papers and was sorely tempted to go back outside, give them all an interview and be done with it. But I didn't. I didn't have the courage and didn't know what to say anyway.

I knew, though, that I had to find my own place now. I couldn't put my housemates through any of this. Apart from anything else, they didn't know about the money and just treated me like one of them, which was exactly how I liked it. But now everybody would know about my fortune. And I wasn't sure if I could cope with that. Then, however, I remembered that it was near the beginning of the long summer vacation and, hopefully, by the time the students came back, it would all have blown over. I was, however, determined now to find my own little bolthole, one where I would be difficult to trace. But how would I go about doing that? Perhaps the first thing to do was to visit an estate agent. They might have some ideas.

So I decided to put this plan into action at once. I got a few addresses from the internet and went out through the back garden and into the lane behind the house. There was nobody there and I breathed a sigh of relief. I needed a taxi and found one quite quickly cruising down the main road. Giving the driver the address of the first estate agent on the list, I sat back and tried to relax although my mind was churning.

We soon got there and I went in and was greeted by a nice young woman who took my jacket and offered me coffee. I explained that I had an abusive boyfriend (an idea I'd had in the taxi) and I needed a place quickly which I could enter and leave without being spotted. Either to buy or to rent, I said. She was very sympathetic but told me they had nowhere on their books at present which would suit me. I told her that I'd owned a house outright, which had been given to me by my parents, but had recently sold it, so money was no problem but I did need a new place fast. She sat back in her chair and looked at me speculatively.

Then she said, 'Let me make a couple of phone calls. I know most of the estate agents in the city.' I sat there and sipped my coffee while she made her calls but quite quickly she put the phone down and said, 'I have a mate in another estate agent's who may be able to help you. He says he has the kind of place you need but it *is* expensive.'

'Don't worry about that,' I said. 'I told you I have money there in my bank account.'

'Yes, I know you did,' she said. 'Well, I'm sending you to him now. He says the property is available immediately.'

'Great,' I said. 'Can you call me a taxi, please?' It wasn't difficult to act paranoid.

'Yes, of course. Here's the name and address,' and she scribbled something on a piece of paper.

The taxi came quickly and I thanked the woman, who said, 'Good luck,' and gave me a genuine woman-to-woman smile.

I left and went straight to the other estate agent who was a youngish, quite good-looking guy, dressed smartly. He introduced himself as Graham and took me through to his office. When we were both seated, he said, 'Madeleine has explained the situation to me and I understand your reason for the rush. Here are the property's details.' And he handed me a portfolio with a picture on the front of a detached house. I didn't recognise the address and asked him where it was.

'Actually, not far from here,' he said. 'Estate agents like to keep their business close to their office if they can. It's tucked away at the end of a cul-de-sac and the house is divided into two flats. The first floor one has its own entrance round the back of the property and that's the one that's come up for sale.

'It sounds ideal,' I said enthusiastically. 'Can I see it?'

'Don't you want to look at the details first?'

'I'll look at them on the way over,' I said.

So we went outside and got into his car and he took me over to the property. On the way, I asked who lived in the ground floor flat and he said it was an elderly gentleman who kept very much to himself. Better and better, I thought to myself. What he'd said was true enough. It wasn't far from his office and I spent the journey looking at the details of the house. It sounded fantastic to me but then I remembered from watching programmes on TV that estate agents always made their houses sound more attractive than they actually were. I wondered how long it would take for me to cycle from there to uni and I reckoned that, actually, it shouldn't take much longer than it did now.

We parked out at the front and Graham took me round the back of the house to where there was a small garden with an exterior staircase leading up to the first floor. I asked whether it was necessary to come from the front and he said no and showed me the back gate to the garden which led onto a small lane which seemed to curve just beyond the house. I asked where the lane led and he said, 'Back to the main road.'

Then we went up the stairs to the front door of the flat which he opened. I was stunned by the beauty of the interior. It was even more wonderful than the pictures in the portfolio. There were two good-sized bedrooms, a large lounge-cum-dining area with a huge window looking out over the garden, a smallish kitchen which seemed to have every gadget known to man in it, and a very clean bathroom with a proper bath and shower in it. Fortunately, the gas, water and electricity were still on and I asked him why. He said it was because he had to show prospective buyers around and they didn't want to come into a cold flat with no lights. But he told me that I would have to get these things sorted out sooner rather than later if I wanted the place and I said distractedly, 'Yes, of course.' However, I'd already decided.

'Why hasn't this place been snapped up already?' I asked.

'Well, it hasn't been on the market long and the exterior staircase makes it rather eccentric,' he told me.

'I'll take it,' I said.

'What?' he said. 'Just like that?'

'Yes, just like it is,' I replied with a smile, deliberately misinterpreting what he'd said. 'What's the absolute quickest way to get the keys?'

'Have you got the cash on you?' he asked jokingly.

'No, but it's only a phone call away.'

'Okay,' he said, more seriously. 'You make your phone call and ask for the money to be sent to the following account.' And he took a card out of his pocket and passed it to me. I rang David and asked him to send £178,000 to the account number on the card, reading off the numbers to him.

'Can you do it at once please? It's rather urgent.' He asked no questions but said the money should appear in the account almost immediately. I thanked him and said, 'Ring me back tonight and I'll tell you what's been going on here if that's okay.'

'Yes, fine, Annabelle,' he said. 'I trust you.'

Graham, who'd been listening to my side of this brief conversation, said, 'You must have a very understanding bank manager.'

'Oh, I do. Why don't you ring your bank and ask if the money's gone through now?'

He did this and when he hung up, I looked at him questioningly. 'It's all there,' he said, visibly shaken by the speed at which the transaction had taken place. 'This is very unusual, you know.'

'I don't care. Can I have the keys now?' And he, rather reluctantly, handed them to me. 'You can send round the paperwork whenever you like.'

'Is there anything else I can do for you, Miss? I don't even know your name.'

'I think you'll probably find it out soon enough. And yes, there is one more thing. I want you to swear on whatever you hold most sacred that you will not tell anyone where I am, not even if they offer you quite a lot of money. Oh, and don't worry. I'm not a bank robber on the run from the police.'

He smiled at me then and said, 'I didn't think you were. And yes, I swear.'

'Thank you, Graham. I think you might just have saved my life.'

'Do you want a lift back to the office?'

'No, I just need a taxi.'

'I'll take you to where you can find one.' Then he added, 'Do you think we could meet again outside of strange transactions?'

'Maybe. I'll see,' I replied.

So we left my new flat, but not before he'd shown me how the heating worked and where the instruction booklets for the appliances were kept, and went back to the main road where there were a number of useful shops. I found a taxi quickly and asked the driver to take me back to my student house. At my direction, we went past it slowly but there was no sign of the reporters. I asked him to wait and went inside. Once safely there I quickly packed the things I thought I'd need for the first night in my new place, including bedding, deciding to come back for everything else later. I put the lot, including all the cash I had left, in a couple of large, empty cardboard boxes I found and lugged them downstairs and out to the waiting taxi. Then I asked the driver to take me back to the main road where he'd picked me up. When we got there, I told him to go a little further down to the end of the lane behind my house. There I got out and paid him, leaving a biggish tip but not so big that he would remember me easily.

I dragged the boxes down the lane and up to my new flat and sat on the empty floor, shattered by everything I'd accomplished. But I knew I couldn't rest yet. I had to buy some furniture and some food. I thought I'd seen a furniture shop on the main road along with a small supermarket so I wearily got to my feet and trudged out again but not before changing into one of my hoodies. I didn't want to be easily remembered by the locals. It still hadn't sunk in what I'd done – actually bought my very own place. I knew money talked and here was living proof!

Anyway, I went out and bought all the essentials I knew I needed and got a promise from the furniture people that they'd deliver later in the day. Then I went home, weighed down with shopping bags, and collapsed again on the floor. I actually went to sleep for a bit but was woken by the trilling of my mobile phone. Blearily I picked it up and was relieved to see it was David.

I explained briefly all that had happened the past few days and he congratulated me on my exam results, like Peter had done, and said that I'd shown great initiative evading the reporters. He added, 'I guessed the money was for a property of your own and I'm very pleased you've got one now. It was about time.'

I thanked him and hung up. Then I realised I needed a shower so I went into the bathroom and decided to have a long, hot soak in the tub instead. I felt much better when I got out but was positively starving as I'd missed lunch. So I cooked myself a simple meal in the kitchen and ate it sitting on the empty floor of the living room. I was just wondering when the furniture would arrive when the doorbell chimed and I went down to the front to find a large van parked outside. I directed the men to bring everything round to the back, where they climbed the staircase and brought it all in. Then they left with my thanks and I positioned everything where I thought it looked best. Now I actually had a bed to sleep in and I made it up with my own sheets and duvet which I'd brought from the old house. Then I just collapsed onto it and went to sleep, fully-clothed.

And that is how I bought my first very own place to live.

The following day I got up early as I wanted to go round to my old house and get the rest of my stuff. So I walked up to the main road, wearing my hoody. I knew that I needed some kind of accommodation address where mail could be sent to me without it going straight to the house and I went first into the local post office to enquire about this. There they told me that the best way to do it was to get a PO Box set up and said that a shop just a little way up the road could help me. So I went there next and found it was a newsagent's, run by a lovely

Indian family. I explained what I wanted and they said it was easy to do. So I filled out a couple of forms, paid a deposit and a month's rent in advance, and was told that I could come in any time to pick up my mail. They said I could even have mail forwarded from my old address if I wanted and I said yes, thinking how convenient that was. I wished I didn't have to use my real name on the forms but there was nothing I could do about it since I'd had to show my student card as identification. Then I bought myself a copy of the local paper and left thanking them.

I found a taxi and went over to my old house, reading the paper on the way. On an inside page I found a big picture of myself standing outside my old house with my mouth open, staring incredulously at the reporters clustered around me. I thought I looked terrible, a real mess, but at least I wasn't crying. Then I read the accompanying article which had the headline "Heiress Hiding out in Student House?" The article itself was a mish-mash of made-up "facts" with a few nuggets of hard information buried inside them. I wondered, for example, how they'd found out the subject I'd been studying at university and the fact that I'd just been awarded a first. Who had let that out? Fortunately, however, there was no mention of the business course I was proposing to start in September.

Having packed everything up, I sat in my now bare room and thought about all the good times I'd had in the house but I knew it was time to leave. Then I managed to cram everything else I had, except for my bike, into another taxi and get it all home.

Chapter 14

I knew I had to lie low for a while until the press lost interest and it was then that I had a truly brilliant idea. I'd go on holiday! I'd never had a real holiday in my life. Sure, I'd been dragged around museums all over Europe by Mother when I was much younger, but it was always because she was keeping a beady eye out for possible acquisitions for her art collection and I never enjoyed myself. During my three years at uni I'd spent every holiday working in the bar, so I'd never done anything purely for my own enjoyment. I decided then and there that I'd go somewhere warm where there was no possibility of anybody recognising me and just laze around for a couple of weeks. It sounded brilliant! I knew that David wouldn't begrudge me the money I'd need. After all, it was mine and I felt I'd earned a holiday.

So, after checking there were no reporters hanging around, I went back to my old house for the last time and got my bike, picking up my mail on the way out. From there I peddled over to the university administration building and handed in my keys, telling them I'd moved house but that where I was living now had to be kept secret. The assistant who helped me asked why that was and I showed her my copy of the morning paper. She understood at once my need for secrecy but said I needed to tell them where to send any letters from the university and I gave her my new PO Box address, which satisfied her. 'You'll be a postgraduate when you start the new term and, as such, we will no longer be in loco parentis for you,' she said and I was glad of that.

Another thing done, I thought as I peddled away. But I knew my chores were far from over. The first priority was probably to call Peter and tell him what I'd done so I stopped in a local park and sat on a bench. There, I dialled his number at work and was put through to his secretary who said Peter was in a meeting and would call me back when he got out. The next thing I needed was a travel agency and I remembered there was one not far from the university which was used a lot by students. So I cycled there and was greeted by a heavily made-up woman who sat me down at her desk. I explained what I wanted and she recommended Barbados as being nice at this time of year and I asked where I could stay.

'Will you be going alone?' she said and I told her yes. She said that there was a nice hotel on the island which catered especially for single people. 'But,' she added, eyeing my jeans and hoody and probably remembering that I'd arrived on a bike, 'It is rather expensive, I'm afraid.'

'Don't worry about that,' I said airily. 'How soon could I leave?'

'Let me check,' she said. And her fingers went clattering over the keyboard in front of her. She turned the screen towards me and showed me the availability for tickets and accommodation. 'It looks like the soonest you could leave is Thursday morning at eleven am.' It was Monday and I knew that I'd need a few more days to sort everything out in Aberdeen and I said, 'Yes. That sounds fine. How much is the whole package going to cost?'

She did some more clattering and came up with a figure. It was a lot to spend on a holiday, I knew, but I still felt I deserved it. So I agreed and she asked me how I wanted to pay.

'Is wire transfer okay?' I asked, knowing that my credit card limit wouldn't cover it all. I have always been afraid of going into debt and deliberately left my limit low.

'Well,' she paused for a moment but then continued, 'it's unusual but, yes, that'll be fine.'

'Can you give me the account number you wish the money to be paid into?' I asked and she gave it to me. So I rang David at once and firmly said, 'I'm afraid I need another injection of cash. I'm off on holiday for a couple of weeks.'

'To escape those pesky reporters?' he said.

'Partly,' I replied. 'Here's the number of the account you need to pay the money into,' and I gave it to him. I heard him typing at the other end.

Then he asked, 'And how much do you need for this little jaunt?' and I told him.

'Where are you going? The South Pole?' he said jokingly.

'No, only Barbados.'

'Oh, that's okay then. If you ask them to check their account in the next few minutes, they'll see that the money's been transferred.'

'Thanks a lot, David,' I said. 'I'll be in touch very soon about our other business,' and hung up. While I'd been talking, the woman had been printing stuff out for me.

'I presume you've got a valid passport and travel insurance?' she asked now.

I hadn't used my passport for so long I didn't even know where it was and it was probably out of date anyway, so I groaned and said, 'I'm not sure.'

'Well, you'd better make sure, hadn't you?' the woman said, sounding rather cross. 'Otherwise I won't be able to sell you a ticket.'

'Is there time for me to get a new passport?' I asked.

'You can apply for an emergency one. That only takes a couple of days. You're lucky, we have a local office quite near here.'

'Okay. Hold everything,' I said and she gave me directions.

I jumped on my bike and cycled as fast as I could over to a big intimidating building which had a large number of government offices in it. I spotted "Passports" and went up a flight of stairs to a rather shabby office where there were a number of people waiting in line. I joined the queue which seemed to move at a snail's pace. But I got to the front in the end and explained to a young man that I appeared to have lost my passport and was due to fly to Barbados on Thursday. He was sympathetic and said it happened all the time. Then he asked me for my full name and date of birth and typed it into his computer.

'Ah, good,' he said. 'Your old passport has expired.'

'Why is that good?' I asked.

'Because it's more of a headache if you still have a valid one floating around somewhere. Have you got passport photos with you?'

Another thing I hadn't thought of in my rush to escape the country! 'No, I'm afraid not,' I admitted shamefacedly.

'No problem,' he said. 'There's a machine just down the hall. If you go and get them now, I'll process everything and, when you come back, it should all be just about ready for you to collect unless you'd rather we posted it to you.'

'No, I'll wait if I have to,' I said. So I ran out of the office and down the hall outside and sure enough there was a machine there for taking passport-sized photos. It was empty but I had no idea how to use it and had to read the instructions carefully several times. Then, convinced it wasn't going to work for me, I went inside, having put some coins into a slot first. Then I followed the instructions and, lo and behold, after a few seconds it ejected four not bad pictures of me. I took them back to my young man who examined them closely and said, 'Yes, these will do.'

'Thank God for that,' I said and he grinned.

'If you'd just like to wait over there,' he said, pointing to a few rather decrepit-looking chairs in the corner of the office. 'It won't be long.'

So I sat down and started chewing my finger nails in my impatience. Why did everything have to be so difficult? I thought. But I reminded myself how easily the house purchase had gone and at once felt better. Then my phone rang. It was Peter. I told him where I was and why, although without mentioning the reporters. I didn't want the other people in the office overhearing my conversation. But he said, 'I saw the paper this morning and I presume it has something to do with this sudden exodus.'

'Yes, it does,' I said briefly.

'Well, have a good time,' he said. 'Oh, by the way, you remember those interviews you wanted to conduct?'

'Yes, of course,' I replied although they'd been pushed to the back of my mind by everything that had been happening.

'The lady here I mentioned to you is definitely up for it. She said it would be good to get out of the office for a couple of days.'

'That's great,' I said. 'I'll be in touch before I leave.' And with that we both hung up.

I had to wait about half an hour until my name was called and I was made to sign my new document and pay but then I was the proud possessor of a brand new passport. I thanked the young man profusely and he winked at me and said, 'All part of the service, Miss.' After that I was straight out of there and I cycled back to the travel agency, convinced that nothing else could go wrong with my plans.

When I showed my passport to the woman, she said, 'My, that was quick!' but confirmed for me that the money had gone through and handed me my e-tickets and travel itinerary. Finally she said, 'What about travel insurance? You need it to travel these days but I can provide you with some if you wish.'

'Thank you. That would be kind of you,' I said formally.

She typed away for a minute or two and then handed me another bit of paper and said, 'That'll be £50, please.' I paid her with my credit card and she said, 'Have a nice holiday.'

I replied, 'I'll try,' and peddled home, well satisfied with my day's work.

Before I left for my holiday, I invited Peter over to my new pad and made dinner for him. He was most impressed with the place and understood perfectly when I explained about going away for a couple of weeks. 'You deserve it,' he said, 'if only to celebrate your degree.' He also said before he left, 'The place is looking rather bare though, isn't it? If you'd like me to take you shopping for a few pictures, for example, after you come back, I'd love to.' I gushed my thanks as always and he left.

I also found time to ring David and bring him up to date on everything that had been happening and he said, 'My, you have been a busy bee, haven't you?'

'A frenetic bee, more like,' I replied and he laughed. Then I said, 'Can you send those CVs I asked for to my new PO Box?' I gave him the number and address. 'I'll have a look at them before I come down to see you for the interviews.'

'Sure,' he said. 'They're almost ready to send off so you should have them when you return.'

'Okay. Thanks, David,' and we hung up.

I did a few other things as well before I left. First, the next day, a large package of papers landed on my doormat addressed to "The new owner of the top floor flat", which was from Graham and pertained to the house sale. He asked me to sign in various places on the many forms and I did so immediately. He also included a kind of billet-doux, in which he said he'd seen the paper and knew who I was but was much more interested in me as a person than in my fortune. Actually, I did rather fancy him as he seemed sweet and trustworthy, but I didn't reply to him on a personal level, except to remind him of his oath of secrecy and to tell him that I was going away for a couple of weeks. He also told me in his accompanying letter that, after he received the signed papers back, he would be sending me the deeds of the flat and suggested that I should leave them somewhere very secure. I knew I'd have to buy a safe but that could wait until I got back. Then I took the documents round to the Post Office where I mailed them all off to him by registered post.

Another thing that happened before I left was that I met the owner of the downstairs flat. He was out in the garden pruning some of the bushes as I came back from running one of my errands, and turned out to be a lovely old man, who introduced himself as Gerald and who insisted on inviting me in for a cup of tea. His flat obviously hadn't been redecorated for many years and I sat down in his living room on an old-fashioned, over-stuffed armchair, waiting for the tea to arrive. When he came back with it, he asked me lots of questions about myself, most of which I answered truthfully, although I didn't mention the fact that I was an heiress. I told him I was off on holiday on Thursday to celebrate my degree and asked him if he could keep an eye on the flat and he said he'd be delighted to. Then I asked him about himself and it turned out that his wife had died many years before and their children were now scattered all over the world. As I got up to leave, he said, 'I've enjoyed this little chat, Annabelle,' and I realised that he must be quite lonely.

As well as these things, I also got the utilities in the flat sorted and put into my name and even found the time to do a little research on Barbados on my laptop, which I knew almost nothing about. I discovered that, although it is independent, it acknowledges the Queen as the Head of State and has a British Governor-General. It is also quite a rich country compared to most in the Caribbean. The main language is

English, which pleased me since my foreign languages weren't too good. The pictures of the beaches looked stunning and I couldn't wait to get there, as it sounded ideal for what I wanted.

Chapter 15

Got back from my holiday a few days ago and had an absolute blast! I kept a kind of diary in a notebook so I'd be able to remember all the details and that's what I'm using now to type up my memories.

Thursday seemed to arrive very quickly and I had to get up very early to be at the airport on time. I took a taxi there and was rather intimidated when I arrived. It was the first time I'd been there and it was so big and busy! But, after asking a couple of people which desk to check in at, I found my way and checked in without a problem. I didn't have much luggage with me as I prefer to travel light, although I'd had to go out before I left to get some warm weather clothing and a new swim suit as Aberdeen was pretty cold most of the year and I rarely had the chance to swim there.

It was quite a long flight, bumpy in places, but I amused myself by chatting to a man in the seat next to me who was, apparently, in the throes of a painful divorce and was taking some time off before having to return to sign the final official papers. At least, that's what he told me, but I'd learnt by now not to take everyone's words at face value. He asked where I was staying on the island and I told him the name of some fictitious hotel I made up on the spot. We arrived safely and I was greeted by a wall of heat like I'd never known before but, fortunately, there was a slight breeze to take the edge off it. It was early afternoon there and I found a taxi outside the airport which took me to the hotel.

This turned out to be very beautiful and right on a huge and sandy beach. I'd seen the pictures on the internet before I left and I wasn't disappointed, with its pseudo-classical façade and high ceilings with fans turning lazily. I was shown up to my room with great deference by a young, smartly-dressed porter and I was delighted with it as it had a huge bed, something I've always fancied, and just about every amenity imaginable. I collapsed into the bed and slept for a few hours until it seemed, from the growling in my stomach, to be dinner time, at which point I got up and had a long leisurely shower. Then I put on a few of my prettier clothes and made my way down to the dining room.

I gave my name to the head waiter and he asked whether I wanted to be seated alone or with others and I chose the second option. So he took me over to a long table which had a large number of obvious student-types around it who were behaving quite boisterously. He introduced me to the girl on my right, whose name was Mary Jane, and then left me to it. The chatter died down when I sat down and I found myself the object of scrutiny from all sides.

'Girls and boys,' Mary Jane intoned in a strong American accent. 'This is Annabelle. I hope you are all going to be nice to her. I think she's from England.'

'Hi, Annabelle,' everyone said cheerily and I began to feel much better about my new friends. They were all soon chatting away again while they were eating and I had the chance to talk to Mary Jane a bit. It turned out that they were a group of graduate students from Yale who had decided to take a trip down to Barbados to celebrate the end of their MA or MSc programmes.

I had met very few Americans before and as a race I regarded them, like many English people do, I believe, as naïve and unsophisticated with very little knowledge of the world outside their borders. I was, however, very quickly disabused of this idea since, in fact, they were all highly intelligent, articulate people who appeared to know far more than I did about almost everything. I found them exciting company and knew that I would be able to have a lot of fun with them. They'd arrived a couple of days before me so they already knew the ropes and they promised to show me around.

After dinner, which, by the way, was delicious, (mainly seafood which I love) we all went down to the beach where the boys played Frisbee while I and the girls sat around and chatted. They were fascinated by my Englishness – none of them had been to Europe – and asked me lots of questions about my home country, some of which, to my shame, I couldn't answer. I wanted to find out what they thought of America too and learnt a lot from them. It's true that, like the stereotypical American, they were all very patriotic but very liberal too, and I found this an interesting contradiction, something I'd not really encountered in Europe, and they quizzed me about this.

The light from the stars was amazing but when some of the boys proposed building a bonfire, there was unanimous approval. Somebody produced a large crate of American beer and they shared it with me as if I'd become an honorary one of them. Before I left them, they made me promise to come down for an early morning swim before breakfast. Finally, claiming jet lag, I excused myself and went back up to my room, a little tipsy but feeling more relaxed than I'd done in ages. And that's how my first day on the island ended.

The next morning dawned bright and sunny again and I went for an early morning dip as I'd promised my new friends and met them all again on the beach. I frolicked in the water with some of the boys this time and got to know them better. I'd learnt all their names by now – there were five boys and four girls – and discovered that none of them were hitched up with any of the others. There was one boy in particular who interested me, called Jay, who reminded me a bit of my nameless waiter except that he had brown hair, not black. He seemed to be a bit quieter than the others and, when we were drying off after our swim, I made a real effort to get to know him better. And over the course of the next couple of days, I managed to.

It turned out that he came from a wealthy background like mine but had turned his back on the business world against his father's wishes and opted instead for a career in marine biology. I found this fascinating and was sorely tempted to tell him how alike we were but managed to resist the temptation, deflecting every personal question of his.

I knew he fancied me and one evening I coyly offered to show him my room, like the demure maiden I certainly wasn't. He accepted the offer as I knew he would and we soon found ourselves romping furiously upon my bed. It was exactly the release I needed and I showed my thanks to him in the most inventive ways I could. For the rest of the holiday everybody treated us as a couple which I found really rather sweet and touching and, as we knew it wouldn't last, we made the most of our time together. One night, after resting from our exertions, he looked at me and said, 'You really are a mystery girl, aren't you, Annabelle?' and I felt guilty for a while for not confiding in him more.

We didn't just stay around the hotel but, after renting bikes, we went on several long cycle rides around the island – the Americans, incidentally, were amazed when I told them that I cycled around my adopted city and didn't even have a driving licence yet. We also went into the capital, Bridgetown, where I bought a few local things for the flat, as well as carousing in several of its night clubs. On the one wet day we stayed in the hotel and they taught me how to play bridge, which, once I'd got the hang of the basics, I thoroughly enjoyed.

All too soon, however, the holiday came to an end – the Americans went back the day before I did – and I sadly packed my stuff. I would return home with a bit of a suntan, some souvenirs and many happy memories. I promised myself that I would do something similar again sooner rather than later, not just get immersed in the world of high finance, never to emerge. The appeal of holidays was clear to me now which, as I'd never had a proper one before, I hadn't really understood, and I decided then that I wanted to see more of the world and what it had to offer.

Chapter 16

I arrived back to a cold and wet city feeling rejuvenated. Now I knew I had to tackle all the issues awaiting me. Almost the first thing I did after I arrived was to go round to see the owner of the bar where I'd worked for so long. I told him that, unfortunately, I wouldn't be able to continue working for him as I had too many other commitments now. He was downcast for a few seconds but then said, 'Was that you I saw in the paper a few weeks ago?'

'I doubt it,' I replied. 'Why would anybody be interested in me?' and he just accepted this.

He said, 'Well, Annabelle, good luck. It will be difficult for anybody to follow in your footsteps.' I hugged him and we parted on the best of terms. He made me promise to come back occasionally and see him and I said I would.

I rang Peter first and told him I was back and had had a good time. I also said that next on my list to ring would be David and that I should have some idea of when the interviews would take place soon. I'd found the candidates' CVs in my PO Box and would have to find the time to go through them. I'd also found the completed house deeds from Graham and knew I now needed to buy that safe I'd promised myself. So I rang David and asked him when it would be convenient to hold the interviews and he said it was entirely up to me. Once I'd chosen a date, he could set everything in motion.

'Just give me a few days' notice,' he said and I promised I'd get back to him soon and rang off.

One of the most important things to do in my own mind was to learn to drive, so I rang around the local driving schools and quickly found one which did intensive courses during the summer and was prepared to take me on. One thing I liked about them was that they refunded your money if you didn't pass the test. So I booked myself in for the first lesson at the end of the following week.

Then I went in a taxi to a shop which sold safes and bought one which, I was told, was totally secure and carried it home with me in another taxi. It was very heavy but, with the help of the taxi driver, I managed to lug it all the way from the back of the house, through the garden and up the staircase to my flat. I gave him a substantial tip for his help and he was grateful. I moved it into my bedroom and stored it temporarily under the bed, after putting the CVs in it, along with the house deeds and all of my decent jewellery, which I didn't have much of left after selling most of the good stuff to the pawnbroker. I knew it wouldn't deter a professional burglar but it should be enough for a casual one. Phew! Another thing taken care of.

Then I thought I needed to buy a few of the course books on the reading list the university had sent me. I knew I'd be behind the others on the course but, if I could get some reading done over the rest of the summer holiday, I hoped not to be too far behind. So I cycled down to the student bookshop and had a look at the books I needed. Most of them looked very intimidating but, thankfully, the university had included on my list a few more elementary books which I bought and put in my rucksack before peddling home again.

Once there, I sat down and started to go through the CVs of the applicants for the post of my temporary Managing Director. Most of them were very highly qualified people, but I wasn't interested so much in their qualifications as much as finding somebody I could trust absolutely. So I paid as much attention to their "other interests" and the letters of application as I did to their experience and qualifications. I wasn't at all confident about doing this alone but knew I had to get some kind of feeling for them before the interviews took place. There were about fifteen to go through and I made two piles, one for possibles and one for improbables. At least I'd have the chance to talk everything through with the lady from Peter's office before I actually met them.

All of these things took me up to the weekend and I decided to ring Peter again and ask him whether I could take him up on his invitation to go shopping for pictures. When I put the question to him, saying that I'd offer him dinner for the help, he said, 'Yes, of course, Annabelle. I'll come round straight away if you want.'

'Give me until after lunch,' I said and he said he'd be round about two o'clock. I went down to the local shops and bought what I hoped would be the ingredients for a decent dinner, had a shower and changed out of my old jeans into a new pair and put on a decent blouse. I didn't want to wear a hoody for the occasion but instead plumped for a nice coat with its own hood attached. Then I had a spot of lunch and waited for Peter to turn up.

He arrived on time and we went out in his car to the big city museum at my suggestion, as I suspected they had some decent fine art prints. It was strange being in a large museum again. I hadn't visited one for many years, not in fact since my encounter with my nameless waiter, and I looked around, expecting him to pop out of a side room at any moment. But of course he didn't. However, I was right about them having a good selection of prints and, with Peter's help, I bought a few modern ones which I thought would look good on the plain white walls of the flat.

'What else do you need for the place?' Peter asked as we left.

'Maybe some decent crockery and cutlery,' I said, thinking of the chipped mugs and other old kitchen stuff I'd brought from my old house. So we went to a good store which sold such things and chose a matching set of crockery and some decent cutlery which Peter insisted on paying for.

I was cross with him for doing this but he said, 'Look on it as a moving in present. And, anyway, who else do I have to spend my money on?'

'You old sugar daddy!' I teased, having forgiven him, and he laughed.

Then we went home and he helped me decide where to put up the prints for best effect and I agreed that they made the flat look much more homely. After that I asked him to come into the kitchen while I prepared dinner and we talked. I told him more about my adventures in Barbados, but omitting Jay's part in them, and how I'd already had a quick look through the CVs but had decided to wait to show them to his lady before doing anything else.

'Her name's Sarah,' he said. Then he asked, 'Have you fixed a date yet for the interviews?'

'No, but David said it was entirely up to me although he asked me to give him a few days' notice. I'm thinking tentatively of next Wednesday and Thursday. I'm starting driving lessons on Friday and would like to get the interviews out of the way as soon as possible.'

'You didn't tell me you were learning to drive!' Peter exclaimed.

'Sorry. I forgot. Everything's been happening rather quickly recently.'

'Okay. Forgiven and forgotten. But coming back to the interviews, as far as I'm aware, Sarah should be relatively free on those days. I'll ask her on Monday morning, first thing. Maybe you should meet up with her before you decide on a list of questions you want to ask.'

'I think there'll be time enough on the train, don't you?'

'Do you really want to take the train? It would be much quicker to fly.'

'I'd forgotten about that possibility,' I admitted. 'Okay. We'll fly. I'll ask David to fix up the tickets. Is there any information about Sarah he'll need?'

'Just her surname,' he said. 'That's Kurchner.' And he spelt it for me while I copied it down. 'Don't forget to take your passport with you. They need some kind of photo ID at the airport.'

'Okay. Perhaps I should ring David now about all this. He'll need to book us into a hotel as well.'

'It's probably a good idea,' he said.

So I rang David at home as it was now Saturday evening and he took notes of the information I gave him of our impending visit. 'Do you think you can fix everything up in time?' I asked.

'I don't see why not,' he said. 'The plane tickets and hotel reservations should be straightforward. As for getting the candidates together in time, that shouldn't be a problem either. If any of them don't make it, it will show that they are not particularly interested in the post anyway.'

'Okay. So all being well, we'll be with you sometime fairly early on Wednesday and ready to start interviewing in the afternoon.'

'Fine,' he said and we hung up.

'I'm glad I did that,' I said to Peter.

All this while I'd been preparing the food and soon it was ready to put on the table. I'd made a nice salad with some pasta and a sauce a friend at the student house had shown me how to make, washed down with a fairly decent bottle of white wine. For dessert we had cheesecake and cream.

'That was lovely,' Peter said when we'd finished eating. I'd enjoyed it too and felt quite proud of my efforts. Peter asked if he could help with the clearing up but I said no, it wouldn't take me long to put everything in the dishwasher. Then he said it was time for him to go and he wished me luck with the interviews.

'Remember,' were his parting words, 'follow your instincts.'

After he left, I read for a bit, then went to bed, thinking how satisfactory the day had been.

Chapter 17

I got back from London on Thursday as scheduled, having spent the whole of Wednesday afternoon and Thursday morning hard at it. It was gruelling although I imagine even more so for the candidates, even though they were only with us for about three quarters of an hour each.

On the Tuesday before I left, Sarah invited me to her office at the partnership so that we could discuss the upcoming interviews. She turned out to be a delightful woman, in probably her mid-thirties, with a good sense of humour. We got on well immediately and managed to cover a lot of ground before we met at the airport early for our flight.

The flight itself seemed incredibly quick after the long train journeys I'd become accustomed to and it was only a few hours later that we arrived at our hotel in London from the airport by taxi. I rang David to tell him we'd arrived and he said he was taking us both out to lunch. So, after washing in our respective bedrooms, we went downstairs and met up with him.

Sarah had told me she was unattached – too busy, she grimaced – and after I'd introduced her to him and he was leading the way out of the hotel, she whispered in my ear, 'He is rather dashing, isn't he?' which amused me. We had lunch in a good restaurant in the city centre but neither of us drank alcohol as we needed to be sharp for the interviews.

David had arranged for them to take place in a small conference room in our hotel as it was more convenient for us. I'd told Sarah beforehand that I wanted her to take the lead in the questioning, as she was more experienced at that, while I would take notes on the candidates. We'd already prepared the list of questions we were going to ask all of them, although Sarah had warned me that the interviews could easily go off at tangents, which I knew from my own experiences of being interviewed at university. It was one of the topics we'd studied in psychology.

When the first candidate was wheeled in by David, he was clearly nervous. I'd studied their CVs again during the past few days and knew all the basic information about their lives but I wanted to go below that, to find out what they were really like. And that was the purpose of the questions we'd concocted. So without any preamble, after introducing ourselves, Sarah asked him what he liked doing in his free time. The question seemed to throw him; it was obviously one he hadn't prepared for.

Presumably he'd thought that all the questions would be about his fitness to manage the business. He muttered something about reading and playing football and Sarah continued by asking what kind of books he liked reading. He refused to meet my eye during the whole thing and I knew he was not suitable, as I told Sarah afterwards, and she agreed with me.

That was the first of fourteen more interviews we carried out in the hotel. One of the most important questions Sarah asked was, 'How would you feel about working with someone as young as Annabelle?' Although most of the candidates were in their forties or fifties, so much older than me, this didn't bother *me* in the slightest and, if any of them gave any sign of being unwilling to work with me due to my youth, they were immediately put in the improbable pile.

The other vital question which I always asked at the end of each interview was, 'How do I know I can trust you to look after my interests?' And this threw most of them.

Some got angry, asking if I was accusing them of being untrustworthy, while others said simply, 'Look at my record. I was always loyal to your mother.' I was really looking for an answer from left field and one of the final candidates at last gave one. He was younger than most of the others with less experience, but had already got more ticks next to his name than most of them and I prayed that he would say something a little different to my final question. And he did.

What he said, grinning at me directly, was, 'Well, you can never know for sure, can you? But if you do decide to choose me, I'll swear on a stack of Bibles, or Korans, or whatever you want, to serve you faithfully.'

I liked his honesty and sense of humour and grinned back at him, saying, 'I don't think that will be necessary, thank you.'

After we'd finished the interviewing, which I'd found almost as exhausting as doing my finals – it had required a lot of concentration – we thanked David and I told him I'd be in touch with the name of the successful candidate very soon. Then we left the south and got on the next plane going back home. On the way, we talked about the people we'd met and Sarah agreed that almost all of them had the business qualities necessary but when it came down to choosing one or two people, we found we were in total harmony. We agreed that the younger man, whose name was John Morgan, was the only one with the character I was looking for and I knew I'd choose him to be my Managing Director. Sarah suggested letting him build up his own team and I agreed with her on that too. I was pleased with the outcome of my visit and resolved to tell Peter all about it as soon as we got home.

I thanked Sarah very much for all her help and she said it had been her pleasure. Then before we finally parted, she said, 'Why don't we do a girls' night out on the town soon?' I said that sounded like fun and we agreed to keep in touch.

The following day was my first driving lesson and it was with some nervousness that I went to the school on my bike. But my instructor turned out to be a lovely, patient older man from the city with a broad Scottish accent and even before my first lesson was over, he turned to me and said, 'You seem to have real potential as a driver, Annabelle,' which made me feel very proud.

Chapter 18

I continued with my driving lessons every day until I felt reasonably confident on the road and, having gone over all the minutiae of the test with my instructor, finally passed it near the end of the summer. I at once bought a small, second hand car and started driving out into the country at the weekends to admire the magnificent scenery around the city, which I'd not had the opportunity to visit before.

What else happened over the course of the summer? I appointed John Managing Director of the company which ran all my mother's businesses after agreeing on a salary and telling him to choose his own team. I gave him strict instructions not to bother me with trivial, day-to-day problems but to consult me before doing anything drastic – by "drastic" I meant, I told him, anything involving more than £1,000,000 – and I left him to get on with it, believing that everything down south was now in safe hands.

I also appointed David my legal advisor as he knew my mother's business intimately and he seemed pretty efficient at what he did, telling him I'd forgiven him for trying to subvert my original contract by bribing my original lady solicitor. I knew he wasn't a crook at heart and it was only extreme pressure from my dear departed mama that had made him do it. I believed I could now trust him absolutely to look after my own wishes as assiduously as he had looked after my mother's.

I also did quite a bit of reading for my course and was surprised to find that a lot of business thinking was basically common sense, which was a relief.

What did I do for recreation? I went to Peter's house occasionally to see him and Mary, who always made a big fuss of me. I also went out a few times with Sarah and found to my surprise that she knew all the naughty places in town. So we went to male strip clubs and other such dubious places but I always enjoyed myself with her. I even invited Graham out once but, while I found his puppyish enthusiasm for me sweet, ultimately I knew we'd go nowhere, so I dropped him quickly. So it was basically back to celibacy for me.

I hadn't been pestered by reporters since that first occasion and I didn't know if it was because I no longer interested them or because they couldn't find me, but either way was fine by me.

At the end of the summer David got in touch to say that the house had been sold and was being turned into an old people's home. I was pleased that it was being put to good use after all the unhappiness I'd had to endure in it.

So everything was looking good at present. I knew there would be bumps on the road in the future but I hoped I could deal with them.

Chapter 19

Only my professor knew the real reason for my applying for the course and he'd promised me he wouldn't reveal it to anyone. I reckoned that was about the best I could hope for. So I started as just one of about twenty post-graduates on the MBA course and quickly got to know my peers. They all wanted to go into business properly when they graduated, hoping to become either entrepreneurs or to join some multinational company, and most of them had some solid experience behind them. If they didn't, they tended to have firsts in a business degree. So they were quite a high-powered bunch of people but I refused to be intimidated by them. When they asked me why I was doing the course after getting my psychology degree rather than continuing with the subject, I told them that I was interested in psychological aspects of business and that satisfied them. Fortunately, none of them had seen the local paper on the day the article about me came out. So, as far as they were concerned, I was just one of them.

The course itself was hard work. We had to cover a lot of ground during the year it lasted and, as I knew already, I had a lot of catching up to do. But my reading over the holiday had helped me and, against my expectations, I actually found myself quite enjoying the academic side of it. I already knew, of course, from my psychology degree how to interpret graphs and tables of various kinds, of which there were a lot, and also how to handle statistics, which I found invaluable. So, in fact, I wasn't that badly disadvantaged. When we got onto the more practical side, about six months into the course, I found it to be, as I'd suspected, mainly common sense and I could hold my own without difficulty against my peers. There were, however, a couple of areas I quickly found myself weaker on and my tutor gave me lots of extra work on these to help me. So, all in all, for the first seven months or so, everything continued well.

Chapter 20

But then the bombshell struck. The *Sunday Times'* rich list came out and I featured prominently in it. They'd even found a reasonable, if old, picture of me. When I saw it on that Sunday morning, I knew it would be avidly studied by all my peers and lay on my bed sobbing. I really didn't feel like going back to university on the Monday morning and being the object of all that scrutiny and interest. How could I continue to be just one of the gang? And what would happen to me if the reporters found my little bolthole? To prick their interest in this, there was even a sub-headline under my picture which read, "But Where Is She?"

However, I pulled myself together at last and phoned Peter for advice. 'I thought you'd be phoning today,' he said. 'I saw the article.'

'But what should I do?' I wailed.

'Be strong,' he said. 'I know you must be worried about how your colleagues on the course might react but they'll get over it. If they become too persistent, talk to your professor. As for the reporters, I suggest, if they do track you down, which is exceedingly likely, you should prepare a statement for them and accept no questions after you've read it. It might be good practice for you anyway to write such a thing. You are going to have to deal with the press quite often after you take over the reins of the company.'

'Thanks for all that,' I said miserably. 'I know you're right. Can I drive out and see you now though? I feel I'm in need of a little TLC.'

'Of course you can. I'll tell Mary to lay another place for lunch.'

'Thank you, Peter,' I said and rang off.

I arrived at his place in a mess, my hair all tangled and my face still streaked with tears, but Mary took me into the bathroom and watched while I washed and combed my hair (with her own brush!) and said, when I'd finished, 'I hope you feel better now, dear.' And it's true. I did. I thanked her and told her that Peter was lucky to have her and she grinned and said, 'I know, dear. I know.'

Then I went and found Peter who was working in his study. He stopped though as soon as I came in, looked up at me and said, 'If you think I could help, maybe together this afternoon we could prepare that statement for the press.'

'That would be terrific!' I said and kissed him on the cheek.

So we had our usual lovely lunch, prepared by Mary, and then went back to his study. His first question was, 'What points do you want to include?' and I made a few suggestions which he noted down. We worked for the rest of the afternoon and came up with about half a typed A4 sheet. I read it through one last time and pronounced myself satisfied. It was simple and clear and made the points we both thought were important. Then I folded the paper and put it in my bag.

'Well, Peter, you've come up trumps once again,' I said. 'Thanks ever so much for your time and help.'

'Shall I put it on your bill?' he asked mischievously.

I ignored his question and made one final suggestion. 'Could you please e-mail the statement to John? He probably needs to see what I'm going to say so that we don't get our wires crossed when the reporters come after him too.'

'Good thinking,' he said. 'Yes, I'll do it right now.' And we said our goodbyes with me promising to let him know what happened. I felt a lot more optimistic now. When I left his house, I switched on my mobile phone which had been off during my visit and saw I had two messages:

one from John and one from David, both asking me to call them. As soon as I got home, I rang them and they both said how sorry they were that I'd been featured in the paper and asked what I was going to do now my anonymity had been blown. I explained about Peter's advice and they both thought it was good. John said he'd received the e-mail from Peter and was getting the company's PR people involved immediately. I thanked them for their concern and said I'd be in touch if there were any further developments.

However, that night I slept fitfully, worried about the next day, and got up the following morning feeling tired and depressed. After breakfast, I got my bike out and cycled slowly to the university – I actually preferred cycling to driving in the city – pleased it was drizzling as it gave me an excuse to wear a hood. I entered by a back way and was a few minutes late arriving. When I went into the department, everybody was there waiting for me but our lecturer didn't allow any questioning of me, being anxious to get on with the morning's work. So we all got our heads down and beavered away for the next couple of hours, although I felt a lot of strange looks being thrown my way. When break came, however, all my peers surrounded me, saying stuff like, 'You really are a dark horse, aren't you, Annabelle?' and 'Drinks are on you for the rest of the course.'

'Come on, guys,' I said eventually, when I got tired of all the ribbing. 'You don't really think I wanted this to come out, did you? But now it has, I just hope you'll let me deal with it in my own way.' And they backed off. But I knew somehow that our relationship had changed forever. If this is the kind of damage money can do, I thought miserably, I'd rather be poor. At least there were only a couple more months left of the course and I thought I could survive those. I really wanted to complete my MBA and refused to give up now.

I had a couple of special friends on the course, a boy called Oliver and a girl whose name was Irene. I had lunch with them and explained my predicament. They seemed to sympathise but Oliver said, when we'd finished eating, 'I still wouldn't say no to a few hundred million quid,' and I wasn't sure if they actually understood how I felt. But then I supposed that, unless you were in an identical situation, it would be impossible to understand.

Anyway, we went back to work in the afternoon and there was no more chance of interaction with any of my peers as, straight after lectures, I got my bike and left the university to go home. I realised suddenly that I'd never invited any of my course mates back to my place and wondered morosely if I was destined to remain alone for the rest of my life.

So I was not in a very happy frame of mind when I got back but I knew I had to get straight down to work. However, before I could start, Gerald from downstairs appeared at my door. He wanted to talk and I knew I couldn't disappoint him. So I invited him in and he told me at once that he'd seen the article in the *Sunday Times* and understood now why I'd bought the flat and never invited people back to it.

'If I was in your situation, I'd want to protect my privacy too,' he said. I almost hugged him as he seemed to be almost the only person to really appreciate my situation since I'd got up that morning. I thanked him for his kind words but he shrugged them off, saying, 'But I didn't come up to talk about money, but far more mundane matters.'

'That suits me fine,' I said. 'What with my course and my fortune, finance is almost the only subject I get to talk about these days.'

'You poor child,' he said with feeling, but then started talking about the state of the drains outside which were always getting blocked. 'All this rain,' he said, 'doesn't make it any easier.'

'What have you done about them in the past?' I asked and he explained how the house had an insurance policy which was supposed to protect it from things like this but every time he rang the company up, they fobbed him off, saying that in the small print it clearly stated that it was only the main drains into and out of the house which were covered. I asked him to find me a copy of the terms and conditions and he went downstairs and came back almost immediately, waving a document at me. I read it through and finally understood that, according to the letter of the law, the company was right, even though it could be argued that morally they were in the wrong.

I showed him the pertinent bit and he sighed deeply, saying, 'I never was much good at understanding documents, I'm afraid.'

'Why don't you ring them up,' I said, 'and ask whether you can have a new policy which includes all the drains? Have you been with the company long?'

'Yes, many years,' he replied.

'Well then,' I said, 'they should offer you new terms and conditions for nothing. If they don't, threaten to leave them and find another insurance company. That usually works. It's the law of the marketplace.'

'Thank you so much for your advice, Annabelle,' he said. 'I'll do it straight away. I'll let you know how it turns out.' And he left but returned very soon with a big smile on his face, saying, 'It worked, Annabelle! It actually worked!'

It cheered me up being able to put my newfound knowledge to some practical use in the real world and I actually managed to concentrate on my work for the rest of the day.

The following day followed its usual pattern although I felt that my peers were avoiding me if they could, probably because they reckoned I hadn't had to do anything to make my money, whereas they were all going out into the world soon with hardly a penny to their names and with huge student loans to pay off. I could see their point, although I wished I could tell at least one of them about my awful upbringing and how I'd had to literally run away to get to university in the first place. Maybe that would get me the sympathy I thought I deserved but then, on second thoughts, maybe it wouldn't.

But that afternoon, after college had finished, as I came through the back gate of the university, I was confronted by a number of reporters and cameramen all vying for my attention. There was no way I could simply cycle through the pack and I wondered who had let the cat out of the bag but then realised it didn't really matter. At least I had my statement with me and I now pulled it out of my rucksack. Then, standing tall and trying to feel confident, I shouted above the uproar, 'Ladies and gentlemen, can I have your attention, please?' and they all quietened. 'I have a prepared statement to read you, but I will entertain no questions after I've read it. Is that clear?' And the majority of them grumpily nodded their heads. Meanwhile the cameramen were all flashing away, which I found rather distracting as I wondered how I was coming out on their little screens. But I managed to concentrate and started to read the statement:

'As I'm sure you are all aware, my mother passed away last year and I inherited her money. That is why I am now doing an MBA course at the university – to prepare myself better for when I take over the reins of her company. I never expected that I'd have to undertake the duties and bear the responsibilities of being the CEO of such a large business, since my mother and I didn't see eye to eye about many things. And it's true that I've been trying to avoid you lot, as I needed to concentrate on my studies.

'Meanwhile, I have appointed a good man, John Morgan, to look after the interests of the company for me and I suggest you refer all questions about the business to him at the company headquarters in London. As for me personally, I've been trying to live as normal a student life as is possible under my rather unusual circumstances and I hope you will respect that and now leave me to my privacy. Thank you,' and I folded my piece of paper and put it back in my rucksack.

I noticed most of the reporters, who had been scribbling in their notebooks, now turned away, looking rather disappointed. However, one at the back of the crowd shouted over the heads of his colleagues (or competitors?) a question which really took me aback.

'Were you aware,' he asked, 'that one of your mother's businesses in the Far East has recently been severely criticized by Amnesty International for using what amounts to slave labour?'

'No I wasn't,' I said curtly, 'but, as I said in my statement, all questions about the business should be referred to John Morgan.' And then I jumped on my bike and peddled away as fast as possible. I was shaken by this revelation and knew I'd have to check it out with John as soon as possible. If there was one thing I didn't want to inherit, it was an unethical business.

As soon as I got home, I put through a conference call to Peter, David and John and, when we were all on the line, I brought them up to date with the latest developments. Then I asked Peter and David to hang up while I asked John something. As soon as we were alone, I asked him if he was aware of the Amnesty International allegation and he admitted he was and was looking into it.

'How long have you been aware of it?' I asked.

'About three weeks,' he said.

'And what have you found out in that time?'

'There seems to be some truth in the allegation,' he said hesitantly and continued, 'but I didn't want to bother you about it as not very much money is involved.'

'If we're employing slave labour,' I exploded angrily, 'I'm not surprised!'

'Well, what do you want me to do about it?' he asked, rather petulantly I thought.

'Get the company to pay a proper living wage and threaten to close it down sooner rather than later if they don't,' I said firmly. 'I want all my affairs to be squeaky clean.' Then I added, 'And while we're on the subject of squeaky clean, when was the last proper, external audit done of the company?'

The question seemed to throw him and he said after a few seconds' pause, 'I'm not sure if one's ever been done. We've always used our own firm of auditors.'

'Okay. Well, I want you to set one up as soon as feasible, preferably with Sims and Cooper,' which I knew was one of the most highly respected firms of auditors in the City.

'It'll be expensive,' he grumbled.

'Yes, I know but at least I'll know if anybody's had their hand in the cookie jar after it's been done. And also presumably it means we won't have to pay our own auditors next year for their audit.'

'Yes, that's true,' he said slowly. 'Okay. I'll set it up. And actually I agree with you. It's about time one was done.'

'And you'll keep me informed about the company in the Far East and any other similar companies around the world? I don't want to be caught on the hop again.'

'Yes, of course. Your wish is my command, Mistress,' he replied in his usual cheeky way, 'but don't forget if you were here at the hub of things, you'd have known about the company and would have been able to give me instructions earlier.'

'That's what I pay you for, to look after things in my absence, John,' I said now, angry again.

'Yes, I know,' he said, placatory now. 'And it will be done, I promise.'

'Good,' I said and hung up.

Then I had what I thought was a brilliant idea. I wanted to travel and see more of the world and I reckoned that, if I made a round-the-world trip, visiting as wide a cross-section of my company's assets abroad as I could to check up on them, I could combine my desire to travel with work. Basically I wanted to see if all our employees were being paid a living wage and, where necessary, whether their other conditions of employment were satisfactory. Yes, I'd do it, I said to myself, early next year preferably, once I'd got a bit of a feel for the business down south. I was pleased with my decision and reminded myself to tell John about it the next time we spoke. I wondered if my mother had ever done anything similar but thought, on balance, probably not.

Chapter 21

The rest of the course came and went without any other disasters and I did rather well in the end. However, I didn't go to the end-of-course party as I didn't want to be pestered by my peers about my plans or have any of them asking me for a job, although I did say goodbye to all of them and wished them luck.

The reporters left me alone, fortunately, although John told me he'd had interviews with a number of them for business papers about the slavery issue and he'd managed to convince them that he had indeed sorted out the problem with the offending company in the Far East and that it was now paying a living wage to its workers.

Now I'd finished my studies, I knew it was time to pull up my roots and go back down south again. So I sold my bike and most of my books to an incoming student and the flat (at a profit), using Graham as my estate agent. I didn't forget to say goodbye to Gerald downstairs and we had a last cup of tea together. Then I knew I had to say a proper goodbye to Peter and

Mary, so I invited them both to the same restaurant where I'd been with Peter all those months ago. We had a lovely meal and I was very tearful when it ended, but Peter reminded me that it was only a hop, skip and a jump on a plane to come back and I promised I would.

'I wish you could come with me, Peter,' I said, hugging him. 'I will miss your advice.'

'You're a big girl now,' he said, 'and perfectly capable of making your own decisions.' I hoped he was right.

The next day I loaded up the car with all my personal possessions and drove slowly down south, stopping off a few times to visit places I'd never had the chance to see. The trip took a few days but all too soon I arrived in London. John had fixed me up with a pied-à-terre there with a basement garage although I knew I wouldn't be driving much in the city and I moved in, knowing that on the following day, a Monday, I'd be thrown into the hurly-burly of the business world. I didn't sleep very well that first night, being disturbed by the constant drone of traffic outside which I wasn't used to and the unfamiliar bed. So I got up in rather a bad mood the next morning.

Chapter 22

However, when I got to the headquarters of the company, which wasn't far from my little flat, I started to cheer up, being given a very warm welcome by John and the members of his team. I found I'd even been given my own PA and secretary which I'd forgotten I'd need. My secretary was a girl called Sandra, not much older than me, but I found out very quickly that she was extremely efficient and could be formidable when needed. My PA was a youngish man, a very smooth operator, named Simon. So I knew I would be well taken care of.

John said jokingly, when we were alone in my large, top floor office at last, 'Now you're here, I hope I'm going to be able to relax a little.'

'No way,' I retorted with a grin. 'If anything, I'll have you working even harder,' and he groaned.

'So bring me up to date,' I said seriously then.

And without any waffle, he did so. It seemed that during the past year my fortune had increased by another £25 million. That meant yet more taxes, but they'd all been paid on time.

'Have you thought,' he said, 'about moving the company headquarters to a country which has a lower rate of corporate tax?'

'We did some work on that idea during my course,' I said, ''but I'm quite happy at the moment to pay the necessary taxes in the country of my birth. I have no intention of becoming a tax exile, which is what it would mean.'

'Okay,' he said, 'as you wish.' And we changed the subject as he continued to brief me on the important stuff I needed to know immediately. Finally, he said, 'That's probably enough for now. It's a lot to take in all at once.'

'Thanks, John. Are you sure there are no other major headaches looming on the horizon, like the slavery problem?'

'No, not as far as I know. But you never know what's just around the corner waiting to bite you on the arse.'

I smiled at his turn of phrase and said, 'By the way, have you thought any more about my idea of travelling to see some of our assets round the world?' I had mentioned this to him a couple of times on the phone.

'Yes. I think, in principal, it's an excellent idea. But there will be a lot of preparation needed.'

'I'd like, if possible, to arrive unannounced so that the bosses won't have time to sweep their sins under the carpet.'

'Hmm. That makes it even more difficult. But I'll get Simon and our feasibility team to prepare a report for you.'

'Thanks, John. Well, what can I do to make myself useful round here now?'

'You could always make coffee for everyone,' and he grinned.

'I could do that,' I replied seriously, 'but perhaps I would be better employed in finding out more about the people you've hired. Can you send down for everyone's personnel records?'

'That's exactly the kind of thing you can use Sandra for,' he said, getting up to leave. On the way out, he added, 'I'm really looking forward to working with you here, Annabelle. I think it's going to be fun.'

'I hope so,' I said, smiling up at him.

I soon got into a routine where I went in early, did some paperwork, attended meetings and left pretty much when I felt like it, although it wasn't often I could leave early too – there always seemed to be something to attend to. John isolated me from the day-to-day minutiae of the company, which I was grateful for as it gave me time to think about longer term goals. I quickly got to know the eighty-odd people who worked at my headquarters and enjoyed their company. They all seemed to be in John's mould, all relatively young, even though quite a bit older than me, and all with a sense of humour, which I valued.

I knew I could easily spend twenty-four hours a day on the job; there was so much to read and assimilate. But I had no intention of doing that. I wanted to get out into London and find out more about it. I was more or less a stranger to the city and spent my first few weekends just walking around, trying to get a feel for the place. It was far bigger than my university city, Aberdeen, that was for sure, but I slowly managed to get the hang of the different districts, at least in the central part.

Then I knew I wanted to see the sights which drew tourists in their millions, so one Saturday afternoon I got on one of the see-London tourist buses with an open top and went around the city, all the while listening to the commentary. I found it a good introduction to London's history and I knew I'd have to return to many of its most famous sights.

Chapter 23

What about my private life at this time? I knew nobody in the city at all except my colleagues and I didn't want to ask any of them out on the town. I knew I had to keep a certain distance from them but, when one day Sandra, my secretary, asked me what I was doing that night and I replied, 'Nothing special, why?' she asked tentatively if I'd like to go to a rock concert in one of the big halls, adding that she had two tickets but her friend had let her down at the last moment. I jumped at the chance and said, perhaps too eagerly, 'That would be lovely, Sandra!'

So, when I got home, I changed into a pair of jeans and a T-shirt, which felt much more comfortable than my customary severe business suits. We met in a bar near the hall, had a quick drink and then went on to the concert hall. It was one of my own favourite groups who were playing. They were all getting on a bit in age, but still sounded as good as ever in my opinion and, although my ears were ringing when I came out, I thoroughly enjoyed myself. I told Sandra this and she sounded pleased. 'Would you like to do it again?' she asked and I told her that I definitely would. Then we parted and I went back to my little flat.

But how was I supposed to meet new people, especially men? It was the same dilemma I'd had when I was sixteen, although I no longer had my awful mother to contend with. I thought about joining a dating agency and even went so far as making some enquiries but in the end I couldn't bring myself to do it. It was just too impersonal. Next I wondered about night clubs, which I knew were a good place to pick people up but I didn't think I was desperate enough yet for one night stands. What was left?

Then one evening I was skimming one of the free London papers and saw an advert for an escort agency. It read "Nice young men willing to accompany professional women wherever they want to go. Too busy to find a partner? Don't know the right people? Why not give us a ring and let us help? No commitment." I had never heard of this idea before but it sounded ideal for my purposes. I asked Sandra at work if she could find me a decent escort agency and she raised her eyebrows but, when I explained I needed somebody to go out with, she understood and soon came back with a list of three, all reputable, she said.

Hesitantly, I rang the first and a polite young-sounding lady answered and asked me for a few personal details, which I reluctantly gave her. I was still paranoid about my privacy but she assured me they were only for their own purposes and were guaranteed confidential. Then she suggested I came to their office where I could look at photo albums of prospective escorts. We made the arrangement for the following Saturday morning and I spent the rest of the week wondering if I was doing the right thing.

Saturday morning came and I made my way over to their premises where I was greeted by the same lady who'd spoken to me on the phone. She gave me coffee and left me alone in a small office with a pile of photo albums. I wondered, before I opened them, if the men inside would be nude but, when I looked at the first one, I was relieved to see that they were just head and shoulder shots, artfully taken, with a few details on each page about the individual. I skipped through the first two quickly but, when I opened the third, I almost fainted. There, staring at me on the first page, was my nameless waiter! I couldn't believe my eyes but, after studying the picture closely for a while, came to the conclusion that it was either him or his identical twin brother. I took careful note of his name, which was Italian, and reluctantly closed the album.

'I think I've made my choice,' I told the lady, telling her his name, and she said that Luigi was one of their most popular escorts.

'When do you need him for?' she asked.

I hadn't thought through an answer to this question and said, 'Can I let you know?'

'No problem,' the lady replied, 'but we do need at least a week's notice.' Then, after signing a few forms and paying a hefty deposit, I was free to go.

I wandered out into the cold, wet street in a daze. Did I really want to see him again? The answer to that was: yes, definitely. But where would it lead? Would he even remember me? I thought back to that night at the museum when I was sixteen. It was more than six years ago and I had changed my looks in the meantime but, except for the punkish hair style, not by much. I reckoned I was still recognisably the same girl.

Chapter 24

I knew it was time to get a different haircut, one which would make me look more mature and, incidentally, unrecognisable, and on impulse I went straight into the first hairdressing salon I passed and asked them what they could do. The owner looked me up and down and said, 'Yes, I think we can help you. But not immediately. We're fully booked. This afternoon maybe,' and he looked in his big book of appointments. 'Yes, we have a space at three pm.'

'Okay,' I said and I left my name.

I spent the intervening time visiting the Tower of London, along with about two million other tourists, but I found it fascinating and I was in a good mood when I returned to the salon. The owner showed me some photos of beautiful women, all with different hair styles, and asked which I preferred. I chose one with short hair and asked what he thought. I didn't really care much what I ended up looking like, as long as I looked different.

'Hmm,' he said. 'Personally I think this one would suit you better.' He showed me another. 'It's more sophisticated. Your bone structure is good and, if you want to look more mature, I think it will do the job better without making you look like a matron.'

'Okay. That one's fine by me,' I said. So he washed my hair first and this was an experience in itself for me. I couldn't remember ever having my hair washed by a man and I found it strangely erotic, although I suspected the hairdresser was gay. Then he took out his scissors and started to cut off my lustrous mane of long, auburn hair. As he did so, I had a moment of panic. I wasn't really attached to my hair but I'd had it for a long time and wondered if I was ready to take such a drastic step. But it was too late. Most of it had been hacked off already.

Then he swept the massive pile off the floor and started to work his magic. It seemed to take a long time and I dozed for a bit in the big chair but finally he finished and I looked in the mirror. I looked like a different person! But he'd been right – it was definitely sophisticated and I felt better about my decision. Then he asked me if I'd like to have it dyed or perhaps just a few blonde highlights? And I thought, why not. Let's go almost the whole hog. So I told him, 'The highlights sound good.' That took quite a while longer but, when it was finally all done, I looked completely unrecognisable but rather good, if I say so myself. I paid his hefty bill and left, feeling ready to party.

But, of course, I didn't have anywhere to go. So I meandered back home, where the doorman did a double take and said, 'Is that really you, Miss Annabelle?' and I had to reassure him that yes, it was really me. He looked me up and down and then said, 'I like it.'

'Thank you, George,' I replied and skipped happily up to my flat. I had a bottle of wine that night to celebrate my new look and went to bed drunk but still cheerful.

When I got into work on Monday morning, there were gasps from everyone I saw in the lobby and one by one they came up to me and congratulated me on finally leaving girlhood behind. That's not what they actually said but that was how I interpreted it.

When Sandra saw me up in my office, she did a double take and then said, 'Can I have the address of where you had it done? You look fabulous!'

'I'm afraid it's classified,' I said with a grin, taking the hairdresser's card out of my wallet and handing it to her.

Then John came in and likewise stared at me as if he couldn't believe his eyes. 'Crikey, Annabelle,' he said, – he was rather prone to using words like "crikey" – 'you *do* look different but I think it suits you.' I thanked him and he said, 'It looks as if you're going to have the chance to show it off sooner than you expected,' and he handed me a large vellum card printed in italics with "Invitation" written at the top.

I read it through and sighed. It was an invitation to a big gala dinner at the Guildhall in a couple of weeks' time. 'Do I really have to go?' I asked. 'You know how much I hate those kinds of things.'

'I'm afraid you do, Annabelle,' he said. 'All the captains of industry will be there and I've had to go in place of you while you've been studying. I know it's not much fun but you'll have to show your face eventually and it might as well be at something big like this. Why don't you take Simon with you as your guest? Everybody else will be in couples.'

That made me remember Luigi and I think I blushed but said, 'Don't worry. I already have an escort.' They both looked at me hard when I said this but neither of them commented. Then it was time to go to work and no more was said on the subject.

Chapter 25

The next two week passed in a blur of work and shopping. I needed a new outfit if I was going to a fancy do and finally chose a slinky black dress with a pair of nice, high-heeled, black shoes to go with it. I also rang the escort agency and told them where I was going and asked them to have Luigi ready to escort me.

The big day finally dawned and I spent some time making myself up, not so much for the occasion but more for Luigi. I wasn't sure how he'd react when he saw me again but I was praying he wouldn't recognise me. When I was happy with my appearance, I just sat in my small living room waiting for him to turn up. He'd be the first person to see where I lived in London and I'd done a big tidy up. Fortunately, the place was cleaned regularly so I didn't have to worry about dirt. At last the doorbell rang and I went downstairs to meet him with my heart thudding wildly. When I saw him looking exactly as he'd done on my big night all those years ago, I almost fainted. It's true that now he was wearing immaculately cut evening dress but it looked so similar to his waiter's uniform I found it hard to tell the difference.

After introducing himself politely but distantly, I invited him up to my flat for a drink and he followed me. Clearly he hadn't recognised me and I was profoundly relieved. I wanted the revelation to be on my own terms. I asked him how I looked and he said, 'Good enough to eat,' with the cheeky grin I remembered so well. I poured him a small glass of whisky and we chatted for a bit with me digging for any personal information I could find out about him. He was reluctant to divulge much about his past but he did tell me that his parents had been wealthy and sent him to a good British public school but, as he was a second son, he hadn't inherited much from them, in the normal tradition of Italian families. He was doing this job, he told me, to make enough money to travel round the world.

'How much longer do you think it will take you?' I asked curiously.

'Not long now,' he replied in his accentless English.

I didn't want to push him too hard yet and, looking at my watch, I realised it was time to go. So I called a taxi and we went back downstairs together.

When we arrived at the Guildhall, I had to show my invitation to get in and the doorman examined me closely, probably wondering what such a young lady was doing at an occasion like this. Everybody else seemed to be in their sixties or seventies, just like at Mother's gala I'd attended all those years before. There were lots of photographers at the entrance all snapping away like mad and I hoped I looked okay. We were put at a table with a number of these elderly people and I was amazed when one of my neighbours called out to Luigi, 'Good to see you again, Lew. How are you?'

'Fine, thanks, Lady Albisham,' he replied and proceeded to introduce me around the table. He appeared to know most of the people there, especially the women, which really astonished me, and seemed to be popular with all of them. I congratulated myself on my choice of escort, especially as everybody was nice to me and kept making comments like, 'Are you going to make Lew settle down at last?' to which I didn't have a satisfactory reply. But I smiled a lot which seemed to do the trick.

The food came at last and I busied myself eating. My neighbours didn't seem to have realised that he was *my* guest at the occasion and I was perfectly happy to keep that impression going. The more people who thought that I was just Luigi's piece of skirt, the better, as far as I was concerned. We finished eating and the speeches began. I was determined not to doze off during them and just about managed to keep awake and clap at the right moments. And finally it was all over and we could leave.

But then one of the bigwigs who had made a speech came up to me, held out his hand and said, 'You must be the new CEO of your mother's company. I'd heard you'd taken over the reins. You really do look remarkably like her,' and my heart sank. My secret was out and I couldn't deny it. We talked for a few minutes, mainly about how the new government was going to influence the business world, and I think I managed to hold my own, while Luigi just stood there waiting patiently in the background. Finally I made my excuses and fled with Luigi hot on my heels. When we got outside, we had to run the gauntlet of yet more photographers and I had to endure more flashing light bulbs but we managed in the end to get away.

Luigi asked then, 'And what would you like to do now, Miss Annabelle?'

'I'd like to go dancing,' I replied and it was true. 'Do you know anywhere civilised?'

'Of course I do,' he said. And we piled into a waiting taxi. He took me to a very discreet nightclub where the music was loud enough to dance to but not so loud that you couldn't hear yourself speak and between dances I asked him how come he'd known so many of the people at the Guildhall.

He laughed and said, 'When you've been doing this job as long as I have, you naturally get to meet people at the top of all sorts of professions although I was surprised myself to be seated at a table where I knew so many of the guests.'

'How many other single women are out there though like me?' I asked.

'Plenty,' was his answer, 'if you know where to look. But, remember, it's not only single women I escort – it's also married ones, as was the case tonight. Female emancipation has arrived or hadn't you noticed?'

'No, not really,' I said. 'I guess I haven't been here long enough. But it would be really nice to meet some of them with whom I could exchange experiences.'

'Ask at the office,' he said. 'It's another service we provide.'

'Okay. I'll do that if I can find the time,' I said determinedly.

We had a few more dances, some of them slow when he held me very close which felt good, but I knew what I really wanted. So we left and I invited him back to my flat for a nightcap. When we were sitting on my sofa, I turned to him and said, 'You don't know why I asked for you specifically, do you, Luigi?'

'I've no idea,' he replied, 'except that I presume you liked my looks.'

'Think back a bit more than six years, to a dinner at a big museum in St Albans,' I commanded. 'Does anything come to mind? You were a waiter then.'

He looked puzzled but then the light dawned and he looked at me in astonishment. 'That was you,' he breathed.

'Yes,' I said simply.

'Well, it's a bit too late for apologies, don't you think?' he said angrily. And he got up to go but I restrained him.

'I don't want apologies. I want a repeat of that night,' I said boldly.

He looked at me carefully now and said, 'Are you sure?'

'Absolutely,' I told him, 'but in the relative comfort of my bed rather than in some anonymous toilet.'

'Well, I guess the customer's always right,' he said, grinning at me.

I grinned back and hauled him off to my bedroom where we quickly undressed and got down to it. He was every bit as tender as I remembered and I had a glorious night, coming again and again until I begged for mercy. His penis never seemed to tire and I wondered if he was on Viagra or something. We kept going until the light was beginning to dawn outside and at one point he said, 'You've learnt a lot since that night, haven't you?' but I just pulled him down on top of me again. Finally, however, he said, 'I'm shattered. I need to get home and get some shut-eye,' and I let him go. We kissed before he left and that was almost as nice for me as all the sex we'd had. 'Can I see you again?' he asked.

I said, 'I'm not sure. Let's wait and see.' I knew I wanted to see more of him but I thought it would be better to keep him on tenterhooks for a while.

After he'd gone, I had a long, hot shower, luxuriating in the feel of the water against my skin, and then just went back to bed and slept the next eight hours straight through, waking up only in time for dinner the next day and feeling better, at least physically, than I'd done in ages.

Chapter 26

The next day, Monday, the external audit was due to start and the auditors had been given a large empty office near my own. We met them in the boardroom and they presented us with a very long list of things they had to look at. After that it was pandemonium with everybody scuttling around trying to find all the documents they required. I wasn't needed so I just sat in my office and caught up on more reading and paperwork. At one point John came in, armed with a number of Sunday's papers, which I hadn't got around to seeing, and asked how the gala had gone and I just grimaced and said, 'Boring, as I'd expected.'

'I guess you haven't had a chance to see these after the debaucheries of Saturday night,' he said with a grin, dumping the papers on my desk.

I blushed but ignored his comment, just saying, 'No, you're right.'

'Well, you're famous again,' he said. 'Look at page seven.' He passed one of the papers, a tabloid, over to me.

I turned to the relevant page and saw it was devoted to gossip. There was a reasonable picture of myself taken at the gala with Luigi hovering in the background. The headline read, "Doesn't the Heiress Look Glam?" and under it a subsidiary one, saying "But who's her beau?" The short article accompanying it just repeated the facts about my having recently taken over stewardship of my mother's company and speculated on Luigi's identity.

I groaned but John said, 'I know it's hard for you but any decent publicity is good for the company. The other papers all say much the same.'

I knew it was the end of my anonymity but I also knew that it had been inevitable. I'd have to take to wearing a hood again when I was outside, I thought, but that was the only precaution I could think of. I told John that I would be giving no interviews, especially this week with the audit going on, and he said that was fine.

The week continued, with me going out less frequently, but I hadn't been recognised yet and I was pleased that my hood idea seemed to be working. At least nobody had found out where I lived – or I presumed they hadn't. That would have been too much to handle. George, my doorman, had strict instructions not to admit anybody who wanted to speak to me unless he'd cleared it with me first.

The audit finally finished and we met in the boardroom again for the auditors' final report. They said that, apart from a few thousand pounds missing from one of the company's bank accounts, they had discovered nothing untoward. My chief accountant, a chap called Chris, almost had an apoplectic fit when he heard about the missing money, taking it as a personal affront, but was reassured by the auditors that it was frequently impossible to track down all the money in such a complex business. They recommended keeping an eye on the account to see if any further money went missing and Chris promised he would. Then they signed their copy of the report and I signed mine for the company and they left to sighs of relief all round. But I was pleased it had been done as I was determined that everything about the company should be squeaky clean.

The next thing that happened at work was the handing in of the feasibility study on my proposed trip. I read this carefully and with great interest. There seemed to be general agreement that it was, in theory, a good idea, although my board of directors was not so keen on having their CEO disappearing off to remote regions of the Earth, what with the possibility of kidnap or other terrible things happening to me. They begged me to send somebody senior, but not myself. However, I could not be swayed on this. It had been my idea and I was going to see it through. It would be a one-time adventure for me and they finally caved in. The study came with an itinerary and I looked at this with special interest.

To get the most representative cross-section of our assets abroad, I would start off by going to India and Sri Lanka before going on to the Far East, including Thailand, Cambodia, China and Indonesia. From there I would head south to Australia and then fly across the Pacific to Latin America where the company had a lot of interests and finally up to the mining concern in the wilds of Canada before coming home. They reckoned the whole trip would take about six weeks but I insisted on doubling that, as I wanted to see the tourist places along the way.

I knew I wanted to take Simon with me as he was unattached and I wanted also to take Sandra, who likewise was single, as I knew she would be invaluable. I thought the three of us made a pretty good team and it would mean leaving John behind to look after things in my absence with none of his old team being disturbed. I put the suggestion to him and he looked despairingly at me, saying, 'Whatever I say won't make the slightest bit of difference, will it?' and I agreed. So, reluctantly, he gave the whole idea his blessing.

Then I had to tell Simon and Sandra that the three of us would be leaving the country in a couple of months for about twelve weeks. They were horrified at first but, when I told them it wouldn't be all work as we'd be visiting the famous tourist sites along the way, they both became very enthusiastic.

'There will be a lot to do,' Simon said.

And I replied, 'I want you, Simon, working solely on the preparations from now on. We will need the plane tickets, visas, hotel bookings, interpreters and possibly armed guards in some places. As for yourselves, check that your passports are up to date and that you've got all the required vaccinations. I don't want any of us getting sick.'

'Okay, Mistress,' Simon said.

'And don't call me mistress,' I snapped. 'Use my name.'

'Sorry, Annabelle.'

'Okay. Now run along and get started. Oh, and I want us to fly first class whenever possible. I don't want to arrive at our destinations all frazzled.'

And he left. I knew the preparations were in good hands. Simon was nothing if not efficient at things like that. I was starting to get excited about the trip and made a mental list of all the things I needed to do, including getting enough warm and cold weather clothes as we would be heading into very different climates and guide books for each of the countries we'd be visiting. And, of course, getting my own vaccinations done. Sandra too was excited and found it difficult to apply her normally awesome powers of concentration to our day-to-day work but I didn't criticise her for it.

I saw Luigi once more before I left, this time not to take him to anything special but just to have hot sex at my flat. I was afraid I might be getting tired of him but I most certainly was not – not of his body anyway. I couldn't get enough of it and he seemed to feel the same way about mine. I liked the lack of commitment between us and he said whatever was okay by me was okay by him too. He seemed genuinely sad when I told him I was going abroad for three months and that somehow pleased me. 'You must have hundreds of girls at your beck and call,' I said.

'Yes, but none of them are like you, Annabelle,' he replied. 'Don't forget about me, will you?' and I told him there was no chance of that.

'You were my first, remember,' I said.

Then, as the day of departure loomed ever nearer, I did forget about him as I was so busy tying up loose ends at the company and doing research for the trip. The day, however, seemed to arrive all too quickly and John came to see us off at the airport. He said to me, almost pleadingly, 'Please be careful, Annabelle,' and to Simon and Sandra, 'Make sure you look after her well. We need her back in one piece.'

Chapter 27

And the next thing I knew we were flying over Europe on our way to Mumbai. First class was certainly comfortable and I managed to doze most of the way. I didn't have any of the alcohol on offer as I knew it was dehydrating and stuck to water. I noticed that the other two did the same.

Then, before I knew it, we'd landed and were immediately thrust into the heat, mayhem, noise, smells and colours of India. We took a taxi to our hotel, a good one in the centre of the city, and I spent the entire journey looking out of the window at the sights. It was like nowhere I'd ever been and, although I'd read about it, to see it in the flesh, so to speak, was quite a different experience.

When we got to the hotel, we were asked the purpose of our visit, as we'd been at the airport, and I said firmly, 'Business,' since that was still my primary goal. Then we were shown up to our rooms and I arranged to meet the other two in a couple of hours to see something of the city before we had dinner. I had a shower and then relaxed for a while in the air conditioning before putting on my lightest clothes. We met up in the lobby and called a taxi. While we were waiting for it, I asked the doorman which market would be the best to visit as I loved markets. He wrote down the name of one which he said was safe and said in his lovely, lilting Indian English, 'But you must still be careful, Miss.' I had the few rupees I was carrying and my credit card in a bum bag under my clothes and promised him I would.

Then we were whisked off and the market exceeded my wildest expectations. It was huge and sold just about everything imaginable. I spent a long time in the spice area just wandering around, inhaling the wonderful smells. I wanted to get my friends a present each and we went to a sari shop where I bought a lovely silk sari for Sandra and one for myself. The shopkeeper even showed the two of us how to tie them. Then we went to the leather area where I asked Simon to choose something for himself and he chose a tooled leather belt. Our shopping done, we walked around a bit more until we started to feel peckish. I was sorely tempted to try some of the delicious-looking – and smelling – cooked food that was on offer but knew from my reading that would be exceedingly unwise, so we found ourselves another taxi and made our way back to our hotel.

I thanked the doorman for his market recommendation and asked him this time if he knew of any good restaurants in the immediate area of the hotel. He pointed up the road to where there was a big neon sign above some kind of restaurant. 'That place is very popular with many of our visitors,' he said and I thanked him again. So we walked up the street and into the cool of an immaculately clean restaurant with linen napkins on the tables and candles.

'Will this do?' I asked the other two.

Simon said, 'Sure. It looks great,' and Sandra nodded her agreement.

So we asked for a table and were sat near the window at the front where we could look out into the street. Then we were given menus which were dauntingly large, although, having ignored all the European dishes on offer and skipped to the Indian ones, in the end with the help of the waiter, it wasn't too difficult to make our choices. We ordered Indian beer while we were waiting for the food to arrive and just chatted about our impressions of the country so far. They agreed with me that it was quite different from their expectations but absolutely fascinating.

The food came quite quickly and the flavours just about blew my mind. I was used to Indian food in England but this tasted quite different from a typically English Indian meal. I had asked for lamb curry but nothing too hot and indeed it wasn't too hot but, by God, was it tasty! We washed it all down with more beer and then asked for the bill, as the quantities had been huge and none of us had room for a dessert. When it came, I did a quick conversion in my head and was shocked by how cheap it was. I went to bed early, tired but happy, since I knew we had to get up early the next day if we were to visit the two companies in the city we had controlling interests in, as was the plan.

We met the interpreter the next morning in the breakfast bar as Simon had arranged. She was a petite little thing, called Sringita, wearing a sari of her own, and I was pleased that Sandra and myself had decided to wear ours, although I wasn't a hundred per cent sure if mine was tied correctly. Simon had already told us that she was a graduate student from the university and she spoke perfect English, although with an Indian accent. She already knew why we were here and she approved of my idea to check up on the workers' conditions. Then we all piled into a taxi which took us way out into the city's suburbs, quite a different scene from those we'd witnessed so far. It was clear that out here there was real poverty and I wondered how many foreigners came out this way.

Arriving at the gate to the factory, which made cotton clothes for overseas markets, we were made to wait for a few minutes while our credentials were checked but were then allowed through with a flourish by the guard. We were met inside the gate by the boss himself who seemed very flustered at our sudden appearance, which was exactly as I'd planned it. I asked first to be shown around and we all trooped after him into the factory, which was a huge building, with the most cacophonous din I'd ever heard going on inside. It was coming from hundreds of old-fashioned looms, all clacking away insistently and I wondered what the noise was doing to the workers' hearing. They all seemed to be women with the few men visible clearly the supervisors. Female emancipation had obviously not reached this section of Mumbai. Simon had to shout to ask a few of the questions we'd thought of beforehand and I noticed how the boss deferred to him, but chose to more or less ignore Sandra and me, let alone Sringita. But he seemed to speak reasonable English which was something. Sandra took notes of his answers in her neat shorthand.

Then he took us into his own office at the back of the building where he offered us tea. We all accepted and he sent off a wizened old woman to make it. It was reasonably quiet in there, except for the roar of the air conditioning unit. I asked him what, in an ideal world, he would need to make his operation here more efficient and he looked at me with surprise as if it should have been Simon who'd asked the question. Then I said my company might be prepared to fund some improvements, up to a certain limit of course. That really shook him and he looked at me now with much more respect.

He said slowly, 'Some new machines would be good. The old ones we have are always breaking down.'

Sandra was taking notes I noticed and I asked him, 'And how much would they cost?'

'The newest European ones cost about five million rupees each and we'd need at least fifty.'

'Who fixes them at the moment when they break down?'

'One of the supervisors, but he can only do so much. They are just too old.'

'Okay,' I said, 'I'll look into it. Now I'd like to speak to some of the workers alone, please.'

A look of panic came into his eyes and he said at once, 'No, you can't!'

'Why ever not?'

'You don't speak their language, for one thing.'

'Ah, but Sringita does,' I said, pointing at our interpreter who, until this point, had been as quiet as a mouse. He looked at her as if noticing her for the first time.

'Okay,' he said, 'I'll go and find you a few.'

'No,' I said, 'we want to choose them at random.' He deflated like a balloon. 'Sringita, would you mind going out and choosing about eight of the ladies, please?' We'd rehearsed this beforehand and I hoped I knew how it would play itself out.

'By all means,' she said and left.

'Do you have anywhere we can all sit?' I asked.

'Yes, follow me,' he said grumpily. And so we did until we came to an area which I presumed from the smell of curry was the canteen. It had a number of chairs and tables in it and I asked him to put a few of them together so that we could all sit together. After he'd done that, I asked him to go back and bring Sringita and the ladies she'd chosen in and very soon he came back with her in tow, followed by a gaggle of women all chattering away excitedly in their own language. We all sat around the tables and I now asked the boss to leave us.

'And if I catch you listening at the door, all bets are off with your new looms,' I threatened. He got the message and left quickly.

Then I turned to Sringita and asked her to welcome them all, which she did. I knew I'd not have long to put them at their ease so I decided to be absolutely straight with them and asked Sringita to explain why we were here. When she'd done so, there was an astonished gasp from the women and one of them reached out her hand and grasped mine firmly, saying something I didn't understand. I asked for a translation and was told she'd said roughly, 'We never thought anyone cared about us, let alone somebody from Europe.'

I asked them then, through the interpreter, to explain to me how I could make their lives better and they came out with a long litany of complaints which Sandra duly noted down. 'Well, I can't promise to help you with all your problems,' I said, 'but the ones which affect you all I certainly intend to do something about.' And, after Sringita had passed around her telephone number and told them to get in touch at once if nothing was done very soon, we left the women to go back to their posts and had a quick discussion together about the points they'd raised.

Their most serious concern seemed to be one of the supervisors, who liked to beat the women when they didn't fulfil their quotas and even sometimes rape them.

Sringita sighed and said, 'That's India for you, I'm afraid,' and we agreed that we'd ask for his immediate dismissal. That decided, we went back to the boss's office and found him smoking furiously inside. We told him of our decision and he agreed to do it at once, claiming no knowledge of the man's misdeeds, but then asked me again about the new looms. I told him once more that, as soon as I returned to England, I'd look into it and he had to be content with that. I threatened him once more before we left.

'If I find that man is still around later, I'll have you replaced,' and he blanched. On that note we left the factory and found a taxi to take us back to the hotel.

On the way, we talked about the experience and all three of us admitted that we'd found it distressing but useful. We knew we had another factory to go to in the afternoon and decided to have a quick shower and lunch before setting off again. Sringita left us but promised to be back an hour later. The afternoon's factory made microchips and I presumed the problems would be very different from the garment makers' ones.

And I was proved right. When we got there, we found ourselves in the middle of an enormous science park with well manicured lawns and very flashy, modern buildings all around us. We went into the one belonging to my company and, as in the morning, the management was very flustered at our arrival. But we soon put them at ease and asked to have a look round. The boss took us into the big room where the microchips were actually made but, before we went in, we had to put on masks and gowns and slippers, all of which they provided. He explained that the area had to be kept sterile and we nodded understandingly. When we entered, I was surprised by the quiet and the cool. The workers were all at their stations poring over minute components through powerful microscopes. Again they all seemed to be women and when we'd seen enough and had left, I asked the boss why this was. He explained that women were, on the whole, more dexterous than men and more perfectionist and therefore made better workers for the company than men. That made good sense to me and I nodded my thanks to him.

Then he called us into his office and, after offering us tea, came straight to the point. 'Why are you *really* here?' he asked and, as in the clothes factory, I came clean and told him that my main mission was to check up on the workers' conditions of employment. I told him that I didn't want to be part of a company which exploited its workers and, as before, he seemed surprised that I was the one doing the talking and not Simon. But he said nothing, just nodding at my words. Then I asked if we could speak to a few of the workers and he replied, 'I don't see why not.' He didn't seem to have anything to hide and I hoped this meeting would be less stressful than the morning one.

Then Simon explained that we'd like to choose a few of the girls at random and the manager asked, 'How long would you need them for?'

'Half an hour should do it,' Simon said and the boss, a Mr Singh, nodded again.

'Okay,' he said, 'you can use my office.'

'I'm afraid it will have to be a private meeting,' I apologised. He said, 'That's fine.' As in the morning I sent Sringita out alone to fetch them, as I felt it would be better coming from a local woman, and she returned a few minutes later followed by eight of the employees but without Mr Singh, who'd stayed outside.

After we'd all sat down, I asked, 'How many of you speak English?' and three hands went up. 'Okay,' I said, 'we'll do this in your language.' Then Sringita went into my spiel about why I was there and that, if they had any complaints about their treatment by the company, now was the time to air them. A look of utter bemusement greeted her words and then one of the English speakers spoke up saying, 'Can this really be true?'

I said, 'Yes, absolutely.' Then the women got into a little huddle and started talking to each other in rapid Hindi and I signalled to Sringita to remember what they were saying and she nodded. Then, one of the English speakers who seemed to have been elected as their spokeswoman, spoke again.

'We've decided to trust you and will take it in turns to say what we think about the company.'

Then the real meat of the meeting began and I was surprised by the nature of their complaints. They mostly seemed to centre around the long working hours, which meant that they had very little time to see their families, and also the fact that, as we could see, most of them wore spectacles but the company never helped them with the cost of these and decent ones were expensive in India. When I heard this, I looked more closely at the ladies and realised that many of them wore glasses with the same kind of old-fashioned tortoiseshell frames and very thick glass lenses, rather than plastic ones like we used now in England. The frames in most cases were held together with Elastoplast or Sellotape and I understood how they felt about them.

'Do you have to wear glasses because of your close work?' I asked and, after this had been translated, there was a chorus of yeses around the table.

The spokeswoman said, 'We all had perfect eyesight when we arrived here.'

'Okay,' I said, 'that is one practical thing I can insist on to Mr Singh. As for your working hours, do you have any kind of union in the company?'

After Sringita had translated this, there was a chorus of laughter around the table and the spokeswoman said, 'We are laughing at the idea of a union. Such a thing is forbidden in the company. No high-tech companies in India have proper unions yet.'

This surprised me and I said, 'Well, maybe you'll be the first. You obviously need somebody to support you in your negotiations with management. I'll bring it up with Mr Singh.'

'Thank you, lady,' the spokeswoman said and I sent them all back to their posts. Sringita made sure they all had her telephone number in case they wanted to contact me later and we started our discussion of what we'd heard. I pointed out that nobody had complained about their salaries which I found surprising.

Sringita laughed and said, 'They all have jobs. That's more than can be said about most Indians who live in the city,' and I realised how much I still had to learn about the culture of the country.

'I think it should be easy enough to get Mr Singh to agree to paying for new glasses for the workforce,' I said, 'but how can we put pressure on him to start a union in the company?'

We all pondered the question for a bit and then Simon said, 'Well, Mr Singh seems like a reasonable kind of guy. Why don't we just ask him?'

'Okay. We'll do that,' I said and I sent him off to find the boss. When he returned a few minutes later with Mr Singh in tow, I immediately put the two most pressing issues to him. He wrinkled his brow as he thought about them.

'I didn't know my employees were so concerned about the price of glasses,' he said first, 'but I think that issue can be easily rectified if we use a small proportion of our profits. The second thing is more difficult, but I see your point. They do need somebody to negotiate for them as a group and I suppose that a union representative would be the simplest idea. If I have your backing, I reckon something could be done, although it probably wouldn't end up being a union as you know it.'

'Just do it,' I said. 'You have my full backing.' And we left the factory feeling that a good day's work had been done. On the way back in the taxi I thanked Sringita effusively for all her help. She said, 'It was my pleasure. I would have done it for free, you know,' and the three of us laughed, although I felt she was being serious.

As soon as we got back to the hotel, even though it was the middle of the night in England, I rang John at home and gave him an update on today's work. He'd made me promise to do that and I was happy to talk to him. I told him before I rang off that, if every work day went as smoothly as today, I'd really feel I'd accomplished something by coming out here and he congratulated me. I told him also that I'd ask Sandra to e-mail him with all the details as soon as she'd had the chance to type them up. He knew that the next couple of days were holiday for us and told me not to bother ringing again until I had more work news. I guess he didn't fancy being woken up again.

I knew that there were lessons to be learned from today's experiences and decided to write them down before I forgot them. We had, for example, to focus more on health and safety issues. After that, I looked at my watch and saw it was dinner time, so I had another quick shower and changed my clothes yet again. The humidity in the city was intense and I found myself sweating much more than I was used to.

Then I rang Sandra's and Simon's rooms and found them both in and relaxing. I asked if they were hungry and they both said yes. So we arranged to meet in the lobby shortly. When I got down there, I found them both in the bar sipping beer and I joined them. We had to decide where to go for dinner and Sandra said, 'Why don't we just go back to where we went last night? It was jolly good, wasn't it?' and this was seconded by Simon. So we went up the street and into the restaurant where we were greeted like old friends by the owner. This time I asked him to recommend something for us and he suggested a dish that I'd never heard of but I went along with his recommendation and Sandra and Simon bravely did the same. When it came, it proved to be even more delicious than the previous evening's if that were possible and, on the way out, after leaving a large tip, I thanked the owner, who bowed low and kissed my hand. I wasn't sure what the correct response to this was but I smiled at him and we parted good friends.

Chapter 28

And that was how our time in Mumbai ended. The next day we flew up to see the Taj Mahal and then on to the Golden Temple at Amritsar, the two places I'd always wanted to visit in India and I was wowed by both of them. Like every famous monument, they were much more impressive in real life than in pictures. I deliberately hadn't taken a camera with me – except for the one on my mobile phone which I didn't use much – as I preferred to be able to see the sights with my own eyes rather than from behind a lens, but Simon had his and took lots of pictures, which he promised to share with us when we got home.

Then it was on to Sri Lanka, which again I found a fascinating and beautiful country, quieter than India but with the same kind of problems. We spent a couple of days there visiting two factories in Colombo, which both had a few issues which needed sorting out, before going to a wildlife reserve where I got to see a herd of wild elephants crossing a river, which was amazing.

After this we flew up to Beijing in China, another astonishing city which seemed to be in the middle of massive reconstruction. Everywhere you looked, there were buildings being knocked down and replaced. When we arrived, we went at once on a tour of the Forbidden Palace, which was interesting, but we were really there to visit a couple of factories and we managed to fit these in the next day. Our interpreter there was another graduate student, whose English I found a bit ropey at times, but we managed. We had honed our performance down to a fine art by now and came out of both places feeling satisfied with what we'd achieved.

The next day we flew down to Xi'an, south west of Beijing, to see the Terracotta Warriors. This was a dream come true for me, as I'd wanted to visit them in situ for as long as I could remember, and I wasn't disappointed. They bowled me over totally and completely and they did the same for Simon and Sandra. All we could say when we finally came out was 'Wow!' and I knew that memory would stay with me for the rest of my life.

But then it was time to leave China and head south to Thailand. I knew it was a whistle stop tour of the world and I wished we could slow down for a few days and just lie on a beach somewhere, but that wasn't on the itinerary. We spent a couple of days in Bangkok, dealing with yet another factory, this one making designer sneakers, and it was almost an exact repeat of the first place we'd been in India. We managed a quick tour of the Royal Palace and a ride in one of the small canal boats around the waterways of the city, which I enjoyed, before it was time to leave and head for Cambodia. We were in Cambodia for only a couple of days too but, having done our business in the capital, we headed out for a trip to Angkor Wat which, in its own huge way, was a remarkable place too. Then it was on down to Indonesia.

And that was where we had our first real setback. I got quite ill, having eaten something I shouldn't, possibly on the plane, and had to spend a couple of days in bed. Fortunately, the hotel where we were staying was a good one and had its own doctor, who diagnosed dysentery and prescribed me Western medicine, rather than snake oil which I understood was the local remedy for the condition. The doctor also gave me strict instructions on what to eat and drink: mainly broth. I felt really rough for those two days and guilty about letting my partners down. I knew we'd have to cancel our trip to Borobudur but that didn't really bother me as I was getting a bit templed out by now.

It was more the work angle which concerned me, as we had two places to visit in Jakarta, but Simon and Sandra said not to worry. They could handle them on their own. And they did – quite successfully, I might add. I'd given Simon a letter of authority which enabled him to act in my place and, along with Sandra's invaluable help and that of the local interpreter, they managed very well. I felt as if maybe I was redundant on the trip but then remembered all the fascinating places I was still going to visit and cheered up. I was still feeling very weak on the third day but managed to totter out with my colleagues to see a couple of the sights in Jakarta, although I couldn't stand for long.

The following day, however, I was feeling much stronger and the doctor gave me permission to travel but advised me to take it easy for a while. So, only a day later than planned, we flew down to Adelaide near one of our mining concessions in Australia and spent a comfortable night in a decent hotel. I insisted on going along on the trip to the mine, which produced uranium, and we took a small plane out to it on the following morning. It was a bit scary to have to wear radiation monitors everywhere, but very interesting to see a modern mine working and I learnt a lot. We even got taken underground!

Then it was time to have our meeting with the workers, who were all men this time, very different from what we'd become accustomed to, and the boss got together some of them who were waiting their turn to go down the mine.

They had different concerns from our Far Eastern ladies, mainly about their wages like they would in Europe, although they admitted the management were generous in their terms and conditions of employment. We thanked them for their time – we hadn't needed an interpreter for a change, obviously, although I found their thick Aussie accents and slang somewhat impenetrable at times – and decided there really wasn't much we could do for them. It seemed to be a model operation and the boss was pleased when we told him this.

In Adelaide, a city I liked, we actually got to swim in the ocean on our last afternoon which was a real treat for us, although it was slightly scary being told to watch out for sharks.

The next day we were off to Latin America which was to be the most work-intensive part of the whole trip. We flew first to Peru right across the Pacific and arrived jet-lagged and exhausted, even though we'd travelled first class again. So we rested up in Lima for a couple of days, making it to the gold museum there, which was astonishing, and visiting just one factory before going north up to Ecuador. I was sorry we hadn't had time to visit Machu Pichu but I knew it was impossible to see everything. We had a factory in Quito which I wanted to see as reports had been trickling out for a while of serious problems there. It made sheep and llama skin coats and hats for sale overseas.

We arrived unannounced at the factory as usual and created the usual furore at the gate, but were finally admitted.

By the way, I didn't mention that in Lima Simon had hired an interpreter who was to travel with us all the way up to Mexico. He was a young man called Pablo who was attracted by the adventure of the trip. He told us that he didn't have a family in Lima and was free to do what he wanted. I liked him immediately. He reminded me a bit of Luigi, although I knew there would be no hanky-panky between the two of us.

So the four of us went in and our nostrils were immediately assailed by the most awful stench. It smelled like nothing I'd ever smelled before and I asked Pablo what it was. He said it was the curing and tanning process for the leather. They used very strong chemicals, apparently, and they were the main cause of the stench. I wondered how anyone could work in such an environment, which made me feel sick all over again. Inside, we met the boss who fawned all over us but made the usual mistake of treating Simon as our leader. I told him we wanted a complete tour first and he looked horrified.

'Why on earth would you want such a thing?' he asked through Pablo.

'To see if your working practices conform to the company's rules,' I replied. And, very grudgingly, he agreed to show us around.

So we saw the process of how they cured the raw leather and made it into something soft and supple. I noticed major health and safety infractions almost everywhere I looked, but I knew this was not the time to bring them up. It was an interesting tour but I was more interested in watching the faces of the workers. They all seemed to be terrified of the boss and I wondered why. When we'd completed our tour, I said to the boss, 'Now we'd like to meet with a few of your employees alone.'

He said, 'Very well. I'll find you some of my supervisors.'

'It's not your supervisors we want to talk to. It's your workers.'

He looked aghast at this statement and said, 'I'm afraid that's impossible.'

'Why?' I asked reasonably and he blustered a bit, saying something about how it was impossible to take them off the line but I insisted and finally he backed down. So, as the employees seemed to be mostly male, I got Simon to go out and choose a few with Pablo while the boss sat there glowering at Sandra and me. When Simon and Pablo came back with them, I noticed them all hesitate in the doorway on seeing their boss, with the same look of fear etched on every face, although this time it was even more pronounced. I ordered him out of the room and he left with ill grace. Pablo invited everybody to sit around the long table and hesitantly they did so. I knew we didn't have long to win their trust and would just have to go with our instincts.

'They're terrified of the boss,' I whispered to Pablo. 'Tread carefully.' Then I told him to tell them why we were there but when he'd finished, they all just sat there stony-faced.

'You don't know this but I'm your ultimate boss, not him,' I said, pointing scornfully to the door. 'I have the power to fire him today if you give me good reason.' And I gave Pablo a few moments to translate. I noticed them beginning to waver and continued, 'If you tell us why you're so frightened of him, I promise I'll see that action is taken.' Then the floodgates opened and, although I couldn't understand their words, I knew they were cursing him. 'Tell them to slow down,' I asked Pablo and added, 'If they could speak one at a time, it would be helpful.' And they all stopped as quickly as they'd started. Pablo had obviously been shocked by their language and turned to me for what to say next. 'Just ask them to tell us why they're so frightened of him,' I said. So he did that and I pointed to one of the men to start.

He took a deep breath and said, 'He's a monster, a tyrant. He thinks he can treat us like slaves.' This was filtered through Pablo and I looked to make sure Sandra was taking notes.

'In what way is he a monster?' I asked the man.

'He fines us for every infraction of his stupid code he can think of until we have almost no money left to feed our families.'

'Is this code written down?' I asked. And the man nodded and pointed to one of the drawers in the big desk in the corner of the large office. I got up, went to the drawer and pulled out a sheet of paper with a lot of writing on it. All the points were numbered. I noticed another sheet underneath with many names on it and numbers written next to the names. I took the first piece of paper over to the man and asked, 'Is this the code?' The man understood me without my words being translated and responded. 'Si, senora.'

'And this, I suppose, is all your names?'

He looked at it a moment and spoke again, 'Si, senora.'

'Can you show me where your name is written?' and he turned over the sheet and pointed to a line beginning with Luis Rodriguez. 'What do the numbers mean, Luis?' I asked and he looked questioningly at Pablo for a translation. That done, he scrutinised the list and gasped, then said something in rapid Spanish.

Pablo said, 'The bastard has taken *all* his earnings this week.'

Then I passed the list around the other men and they all looked at it carefully. Various expletives could be heard bouncing around the walls of the room and I said firmly, 'Quiet, please. I think you have probably shown me enough to send this man to prison.' And another of the men said something.

I looked at Pablo and he translated, 'We certainly hope so. If you can get rid of him, lady, we will be eternally in your debt.'

'Can you give me some examples of his rules?' I asked now.

'That list you are holding, Senora, is not complete. For example, last night I was fined two hundred escudos for having a drop of blood on my going home shoes after parade was over.'

'Do you mean you all have to parade in front of him before you can go home?' I asked incredulously. This took a few seconds to translate but, after it was done, all the men nodded their heads lugubriously. 'That is monstrous!' I said, outraged.

'We agree, Senora,' said the man, who seemed to understand some English.

'Okay. Well, thank you all very much for your time. You may go now and you may rest assured that something will be done and done quickly.'

There was a chorus of 'Muchas gracias, Senora,' as these final words of mine were translated and then they filed out.

'Can you translate the list of rules for us?' I asked Pablo when they'd left. He did and they left us even more shocked and outraged than we were already. Most of them were so petty as to be almost unbelievable. When he'd finished, I said, 'Well, we've got the evidence. Now what are we going to do?'

'Fire him on the spot,' Simon said immediately.

'Yes, but who'll take over?' I asked. That gave them pause for thought.

Then Sandra piped up, 'There must be somebody else here who knows the business, mustn't there?'

'Of course,' I said. 'That's the answer, temporarily at least. We should get the workers back in and ask them who they think is best qualified to take over.'

So we did that and after some argument they came up with a name. I asked one of them to go and find the man in question and, while he was out, I asked what the function of the man was in the company. It turned out that he was the accountant and I was relieved that it wasn't just another worker who they all liked. When the man, called Domingo, arrived, I put it to him straight.

'How would you like to take over the running of the company, at least in the short term?' and he was flabbergasted by the suggestion.

But, once he'd recovered his wits, he said, 'Yes, I don't see why not,' and all the men around the table cheered.

'Okay.' I said. 'You're the boss from now on.'

Then we had to tell the old boss the bad news and I called him back in. He appeared subdued, suspecting, I thought, that something bad was about to happen to him. I said simply, 'You're fired,' and he started blustering again.

'You can't do that! I've got my own family to think of!'

'I've just done it,' I said. 'Pack your things immediately and get out if you don't want me to call the police. We've got the evidence of your wrongdoing,' and I waved the two pieces of paper I'd taken from his drawer under his nose. He turned white when he saw them, knowing the game was up, and rose heavily to his feet.

'I've got friends in high places, you know,' he threatened. 'And anyway that lot,' he said, waving his arms at the workers around the table, 'are just a bunch of Communist bastards. They deserve the treatment they get.'

Simon said then, 'And I happen to have the private number of the Minister of the Interior keyed into my mobile phone. If you don't want me to ring him right now, I suggest you leave.'

'And don't even think about coming back and causing trouble,' I said. 'I will hear about it immediately and will send these documents directly to the police. I'm quite sure the workers will back up the evidence.' I looked around the table after Pablo had finished translating and saw them all nod.

He gave up, pushed his chair back and left. I asked the workers to leave too now and check that he left the building forthwith, making sure they all had Pablo's phone number with instructions to phone him at once if there were any problems. And that was basically the end of that saga. I breathed a huge sigh of relief, knowing how easily it could all have gone wrong, and turned to my colleagues, saying a big thank you for all their help, but they just shrugged it off. Before we left, I turned to Simon and asked him if he really had the number of the Minister of the Interior on his phone and he winked at me, saying enigmatically, 'It's always best to be prepared, don't you think?' and I didn't push the point.

We got back to our hotel and I at once rang John to tell him what we'd done and he said, 'I wonder how much he made personally from his little scam?'

'Well, hopefully, it's all water under the bridge now,' I replied.

From Quito we flew up to Costa Rica, but had no major dramas there. We then went on up to Mexico City, where we visited a couple more factories which had the usual disastrous lack of recognition for health and safety issues, the most serious of which, after we'd pointed them out, we were promised would be fixed.

But then disaster struck. Just before we were due to leave, Sandra tripped and fell over an uplifted piece of pavement, twisting her ankle but, much more seriously, breaking her elbow. It swelled up to enormous proportions within minutes and she was in a lot of pain. With Pablo's help we rushed her to a private hospital where they took X-rays and the doctors told us that they'd have to fix a metal plate inside her elbow to let it heal. We found out quickly that she would be out of action for at least the next month and wondered what we could do now.

I decided that she would probably get better treatment in England where she could at least understand what the nurses were saying to her and arranged for a private ambulance plane to take her back there. It all had to be done quickly but Simon, with all his resources, managed it in record time and, a couple of days after she'd fallen, we went to the airport to wave her off. She was taking a lot of powerful painkillers and was really out of it but I knew that, once they'd got her to hospital in England, she should be able to recover reasonably fast.

The question then was: would we be able to finish our trip? But Pablo said he knew shorthand and would be able to step in and replace her. So we decided to continue and carried on up to the Yukon in Canada, our last working stop. Simon only had to buy a new ticket in Pablo's name. When we got to Whitehorse, the capital, it was a real shock to our systems to find it bitterly cold after all the hot countries we'd visited and I was glad I'd brought some cold weather gear, although we had to get Pablo some as soon as we got off the plane.

We took a small plane up to the mine and that in itself was quite an experience. There was still a lot of snow around although it was now late spring and I asked the pilot if it was safe to fly.

'It's never a hundred per cent safe up here,' he said, 'but I've been flying through worse conditions than this for years and have never had an accident – yet.' We were severely buffeted by the high winds, especially once we'd got up into the mountains, and I was very relieved once we'd landed.

We were met by a group of the mine's managers, who'd been told to expect a group of VIPs by the pilot. They invited us into the warmth of their canteen where we gratefully received hot coffee to drink and I explained the purpose of our visit to them. They were surprised but took it in their stride and we didn't even have to ask if we could have a tour of the mine. They actually offered to show us round, which made a nice change. So the three of us got kitted up in miner's gear and headed underground. I remembered the experience from Australia but this time we went much deeper and my ears popped. The mine produced nickel and the procedure used to extract it was rather different from the uranium mine we'd seen in Australia. Again I learnt a lot and enjoyed the experience, although it was tempered by sadness that Sandra wasn't with us. When it was time to get the workers together, Pablo took notes but, like in Australia, they admitted that the terms and conditions of employment were generous, although there were a couple of safety issues they raised which I promised to bring up with the management.

When I did this, the boss said, surprised, 'I wasn't aware that these issues existed, but I will, of course, look into them.' I asked him how often he got to meet with the workers like we had. He grimaced and said, 'Obviously not often enough. I meet with the union reps occasionally but they only ever want to talk about pay, not about safety issues. Doubtless though, if there *was* an accident, which I hope will never happen on my watch, safety would rise to the top of the agenda.'

'Doubtless,' I said wryly.

We had only been there a few hours and after lunch we set off in the small plane, which had waited for us, back to Whitehorse. Again it was a scary journey but we made it there safely. We stayed the night in the city and I got to see my first wild polar bear, which was exciting. The next morning we flew all the way across Canada to Toronto, our last stop on the trip before we flew back to England, and I decided we had to live it up a little. So we went to one of the city's top night clubs where I saw one of my favourite Canadian singers perform. That was a great evening and the next day we did a tour of Toronto. It's a beautiful city and I really enjoyed meeting some of the "local" Canadians who were also on the tour, although they came from all over Canada. There didn't seem to be many foreign tourists around at that time of year.

Our final day had arrived and at the airport it was time to say goodbye to Pablo. Simon had already given him his ticket back to Lima. I reminded him to get in touch with Simon if he heard that any of our instructions to the factory bosses had been ignored. I gave him a hug and in his Latin way he hugged me back for a little too long. But I didn't mind and was sorry to see him leave for his own plane. We had a few hours to wait before ours left and I rang John to keep him up to date with our movements.

On the plane, towards the end of the journey, Simon said mysteriously to me, 'You might want to get dolled up before we land.' I asked him why but he just said, 'John asked me to tell you.' So I applied my make-up carefully and did my hair and, after we'd landed and met John, the reason quickly became apparent. There were a number of photographers there who wanted to take pictures of me. Fortunately, however, there was only one question from them: 'How did your trip go?'

I replied airily, 'Fine, thanks,' and left it at that.

I asked John why they were interested in me but he just winked and said, 'The PR department has been working overtime on your trip and, hopefully, it will pay off soon.' I was too tired to ask more and he didn't volunteer anything else but took us to his car and we drove off into London.

When we got to my flat, I pleaded exhaustion and went in alone with my heavy suitcase. George was there as always and he helped me put it in the lift and take it up to my floor. 'Good to have you back, Miss Annabelle,' he said before leaving me at my door. I wanted a shower before anything else, as I always felt grubby after travelling, so I had a good, long soak until I felt clean again and somewhat more human. Then I unpacked my suitcase and put the few knick-knacks I'd bought on the mantelpiece. After that I felt hungry, so I made myself a simple frozen meal in the microwave. Then I just conked out and slept the sleep of the dead for the next ten hours.

Chapter 29

I woke up to the sound of the telephone next to the bed and picked it up, bleary-eyed. 'Hello,' I croaked.

'Wake up, sleepyhead, and get your butt down to the office. We have some good news for you.' It was John. He was the only person who dared to speak to me like that. He added, 'You might want to grab a newspaper while you're on the way.'

Feeling rather jet-lagged still, I had another rapid shower, got dressed, breakfasted quickly and dashed out of the flat. I didn't bother walking as I usually did but grabbed a passing taxi. Then I remembered Sandra and decided to make a detour to see her as the hospital wasn't far away. So I went there first and, asking the taxi to wait, I ran inside and asked where she was. I followed the receptionist's directions and quickly found my way to her room but it was empty. A nurse came by and asked if she could help me.

'Yes,' I replied, 'I'm looking for Sandra, my secretary.' The nurse said she was sorry but Sandra was being prepped for her operation as we spoke, and she told me to come back tomorrow.

'Do you mean she hasn't been operated on yet?' I said, aghast.

'She's only been here a short time and she's had to undergo many tests. It takes a while to set everything up, but, if you can come back tomorrow, you should be able to see her then.'

'I'll do that,' I promised, remembering that it had been, indeed, only a few days since we'd seen her off at the airport in Mexico City.

Then I ran outside and jumped back into the waiting taxi, telling the driver to take me straight to my headquarters. When I got to the boardroom, I found it full of people sitting around the big conference table with newspapers spread all over it. They looked up as I burst in and I said without preamble, 'What's the good news then?'

It was John who passed me one of the papers, pointing at the headline: "Heiress Returns After Checking on Companies Abroad". It was accompanied by a decent photo of me taken, clearly, at the airport the day before. The article itself was very complimentary, praising my initiative in making the trip and saying that the paper wished that other CEOs would do something similar. That was a business paper but all the others had a similar theme.

'Has Simon seen these?' I asked.

'No, not yet,' John said. 'He's still at home and asked not to be disturbed, but I expect he'll be in soon.'

And, as if on cue, Simon came in and goggled at the assembled throng.

'What's going on?' he said. And John showed him the paper. 'Oh, is that all? It looked like a council of war,' he said. But I could see he was pleased for me.

John cuffed him playfully but then said, more seriously, 'This, folks, is exactly what we needed. We were already a big player but this takes us into the top league.'

'So what?' I asked ingenuously and I thought he was going to cuff me as well.

'Well,' he said slowly, 'if it lasts, it means that we'll be able to get unlimited credit from the banks, for a start.'

'So what?' I asked again.

'If we want to expand, which is the only way forward, we'll need it,' he said.

'Who said anything about expanding?' I asked now. 'Aren't we big enough for you, John? Remember, I've just been around the world looking at only some of our assets and there were plenty of them. Thousands of people already depend on us for their livelihoods. And, anyway, expansion is strategic decision-making and I thought that was *my* province.'

John looked suitably chastised after my little speech but soon picked himself up as he always did and said with a grin, 'Anyway, people, we've got cause to celebrate. Not only Annabelle's safe return but the good news in the papers too. Everybody take the rest of the morning off and follow me down to the pub.' There was a roar of approbation at his words and I realised suddenly why he could make people follow him. He had the knack or the charisma or whatever of making others feel wanted. I knew no work would be done for the rest of the day but I didn't mind. Let them enjoy themselves, I thought. So everybody went back to their offices, grabbed their jackets and anybody else they could find and we all went trooping off down to the local watering-hole in a long column. I told the doorman where he could find us if anything serious happened and followed on behind.

Fortunately, the pub was big enough to accommodate everyone and I got quite drunk that day; making up for the lack of booze on the plane, I told myself, and staggered home quite early, leaving the rest of them to their carousing. There I managed to eat a simple meal, even though I wanted to throw up, and then collapsed again into a comatose heap on the bed, still fully clothed.

The next morning I got up feeling a bit hungover but not in the least jet-lagged. Had I accidentally discovered a cure for it? I wondered ironically to myself. I knew that the first order of business was to visit Sandra so I got another taxi and went back to her hospital, not telling the driver to wait this time. On the way, I had a call from Peter, welcoming me back and congratulating me on the articles in the press and I told him that it had all been down to John and the PR department. But it was good to hear from him.

I went up to Sandra's room and found her inside with two elderly people on either side of her bed. She looked up as I came in and said, 'Annabelle, how good to see you!' She looked much better than the last time I'd seen her and I told her so. Then she introduced the elderly couple to me who turned out to be her parents. They both thanked me effusively for getting their daughter back to England so quickly and I said it wasn't really my doing, more my PA's. They seemed to be in some awe of me and I wondered if they'd seen yesterday's papers.

I chatted to Sandra for a while, telling her some of my news and saying how sorry Simon and I had been not to have had her around for the last leg of the trip. In return, she admitted her elbow still gave her some pain although the painkillers she was being given helped a lot.

'You only had the operation yesterday,' I pointed out and she said that the doctors had told her it'd all gone smoothly and she should be out of her cast in a couple of weeks. 'That's good news,' I said. 'Take as long as you like off. Your job will always be there for you.'

'Thank you for everything, Annabelle,' she said and I left after saying goodbye to her parents.

When I returned to work, I found my desk piled with papers waiting to be looked at and I grimaced, thinking I'd need another holiday after I'd dealt with everything. But I got stuck in and soon managed to reduce them all to some sort of order, the most important ones at the top and the less important further down the list of priorities. I missed having Sandra to help me, although John had provided me with a temp who was reasonably efficient but she simply didn't know the ropes (or me) like Sandra did.

Then I remembered the remark about strategic decision-making I'd made to John the day before and, as this was something I'd been thinking about a lot on the trip, I was determined to put it at the top of my agenda. So I called John into my office and said, 'I've made a decision.'

'Oh, yes?' he said warily.

'Yes. I want you to start looking for suitably qualified women to take over some of the senior positions in the company. I think it's time our company started making use of all the women out there who have at least the brains, if not the balls, of you men. What's the percentage of women at the moment in management positions?'

He smiled at my turn of phrase but shifted uncomfortably in his chair and said, 'I think it's about five per cent.'

'Well, there you are then!' I said triumphantly, knowing I'd proved my point.

'Okay. I'm not going to argue with you on this,' he said, 'or bring out any of the usual macho bullshit about what happens when the women go off and have babies. I actually happen to agree with you and it will be done – as long as I get to choose the youngest and prettiest ones,' he said, finishing his little speech with a grin.

I knew he was happily married and chose to ignore his final words. 'Good man,' I said and dismissed him, feeling that I'd done enough strategic decision-making for one day. Then I buckled down to all the work waiting for me.

Chapter 30

A couple of weeks later, I was hard at work in my office writing up the report of my trip for the board when my new secretary knocked on my door to say that there was a gentleman downstairs who wanted to speak to me. She added that he'd said it was a private matter.

'Did he give you a name?' I asked and she passed me a business card with a name on it, which I didn't recognise, and no business affiliation. 'Find out what he wants and then, if he seems kosher, send him up,' I said.

'I'll try but he was adamant that he would only speak to you.'

I sighed and said, 'Okay. Send him up but stay by your buzzer in case I need you in a hurry.' By now I was used to freeloaders, jobseekers, journalists and other dubious types trying to get my attention and presumed he was just another of these.

She went away and returned shortly followed by a tall, good-looking man, dressed impeccably, who looked about ten or fifteen years older than me. He came up to me, held out his hand and said, 'You've no idea, Annabelle, how much I've been looking forward to meeting you.'

I was annoyed by his over-familiar use of my first name and said rather rudely, 'Who are you and what do you want?' ignoring his outstretched hand. 'You can see I'm rather busy,' I added, pointing to the piles of paper littering my desk.

He turned for a second to make sure we were alone – my secretary had indeed just left my office – and said baldly, 'My name's Michael and I'm your half-brother.'

'My what?' I screamed. 'I don't have any half-brothers!'

'I'm rather afraid you do,' he said gently, adding, 'and, as it happens, I don't want anything from you.'

'Explain yourself,' I said curtly, slumping back into my chair. This had come completely out of left field and I had no idea how to react.

He sat down in my visitor's chair and said, 'My father told me just before he died that he'd had an affair with your mother twenty-three years ago now and that you were his daughter. He'd kept an eye on your development with interest and suggested that it might be nice one day for me to meet up with you. So here I am!'

I looked hard at him and said, 'Do you have any proof of this?'

'No, not really. Except, why would he have lied to me on his death bed?'

I thought back all those years ago to when my mother told me about my potential fathers and realised that what he said *could* be true.

'So why have you only come to meet me *now*?' I asked.

'Because I wanted to give you time to settle into your job. I read about your return from your trip in the papers and reckoned that now would be as good a time as any, especially as I have a rare day off. I know you'll find it hard to take this in all at once but I do hope you'll come to accept it in the end. I'd even be prepared to take a DNA test if you wanted me to.'

I was absolutely flabbergasted by his claim. It was all so amazingly plausible. If it was true, I wasn't alone in the world. I had a real family out there. However, despite my rising excitement, I just said, 'Yes, I'd like that. Would we have to go together?'

'I'm not sure. I doubt it. But I'll find out if you like.'

I looked at my watch and saw it was nearly lunchtime. 'Would you like to have lunch with me?' I asked. 'It would give me the chance to ask the million and one questions I've got.'

He laughed and said, 'I was hoping you'd ask. But it's on me.'

'Fine,' I said, taking my coat from behind the door and following him out of my office.

We went to one of my favourite watering holes in the area and when we were seated, I started to ask my questions, the first being, 'Do you have any siblings?'

'No. Unfortunately, I was an only child, like yourself, I believe.'

I discovered quite a lot about him during the course of the lunch, including the fact that he was divorced with a child of his own to maintain and that he worked in London, not in finance, but in law. He was a barrister, he told me. That quite impressed me as I'd imagined that, if he'd been a conman, he would surely have come up with something a little less checkable. However, I revealed very little about myself to him as I still wasn't a hundred per cent sure of him, but we parted on good terms with him promising to find out about DNA testing. He even paid the bill as he'd promised.

So I returned to the office and carried on with my work but I found it had become difficult to concentrate. What if we were really related? That would be a turn-up for the books, wouldn't it?! I decided then that I would do my own checking on Michael. So first, I Googled his name, using the business card he had given my secretary, and was surprised to see quite a number of entries for him. I read through them all and quickly discovered that he was indeed quite an eminent barrister, a QC in fact, but in the area of wills and trusts, not criminal law, and had written a number of the standard textbooks on his field. He was even in *Who's Who*, accompanied by a photo of himself. And it was definitely him.

So, I could only presume that he was who he said he was and, unless he was suffering from some kind of delusion, there really was a chance that he might be my half-brother. However, I couldn't forget what my mother had told me about the *two* lots of sperm she'd used, which, presumably, reduced the chance of him being my half-brother by fifty per cent. If, indeed, she'd told me the truth on that fateful sixteenth birthday of mine! Also, there was the fact that on my birth certificate, it said "father unknown". If Michael's father had really been mine also, why wouldn't he have his name on the certificate? Unless, of course, he'd been married at the time, in which case perhaps it was simply to avoid embarrassment. I hadn't asked Michael about his parents, only about himself and any siblings he might have had. Something I would have to rectify, I realised. Too many questions, I thought miserably. But then I cheered up at the thought of modern science coming to my rescue and providing answers one way or the other.

So it was in a pensive mood that I went home that day and lost myself in mindless TV until I went to bed.

I waited impatiently for him to get in touch and a couple of days later, he did. He said, without preamble, 'There's a private hospital not far from where I live in Islington where they can do it at our convenience. Apparently we do have to go in together, however, as we are adults, not children. So, when would you like to do it?'

'Can they do it at the weekend?' I asked. 'I really am snowed under here.'

'Let me give them a quick call. I'll get back to you immediately.'

I waited a few minutes and, when the phone rang again, snatched it up. 'Yes, that's not a problem,' he said.

'Okay. Let's do it this weekend then. Get it out of the way.'

'That's fine by me,' he said and he gave me the address of the hospital. 'I'll meet you there on Saturday at ten, okay?'

'Yes, fine,' I replied.

It was only a couple of days till the weekend so I didn't have long to wait. I took a taxi to the hospital and met him in the waiting area. We were expected and the nurse took us into a small office and gave us a few fairly straightforward forms to fill out, asking mainly why we wanted it done. We did this and signed them. Then she asked how we wanted to pay and Michael produced his credit card. She disappeared for a few moments and then returned and, handing back his card and a receipt, said, 'Everything's in order. Follow me.'

We went to another door marked "Blood Tests" and she handed the forms to a different nurse. 'I'll leave you now,' she said. 'Good luck.' We thanked her and then it was just a matter of having a small amount of blood taken. Finally the nurse said, 'It'll be about a week before we have the results. We'll be in touch.' And that was it. Very simple.

We left the hospital together and Michael asked me rather diffidently if I wanted to go back to his place and have some coffee and something to eat. I liked his manner and said, 'Yes, why not?'

'We can walk. It's not far,' he said. On the way we talked and this time it wasn't just me quizzing him. He obviously was curious to know more about me and I found myself telling him about my mother and the unhappy childhood I'd had. He listened without interrupting and, when I ground to a halt, he just looked at me and said, 'That is sad.' And he went on to tell me a lot about his own childhood which had been somewhat more conventional than mine and that gave me the chance to ask him about his parents. He told me that his father had been a businessman like my mother, and about how he'd been sent away to boarding school and how devastated he'd been when his mother died – he had just turned sixteen – and how all the fight seemed to go out of his father when it happened.

'When did he die?' I asked, remembering my mother's words about my parentage from all those years before.

'In 2002,' he told me.

I did a quick calculation and realised that was indeed the year I'd turned sixteen. So what my mother had told me *could* have been true after all. Michael's father could have been the second man she'd mentioned. It seemed as if the whole idea was becoming more and more plausible.

'And did he die of natural causes?'

'If you can call cancer a natural cause, yes.'

'How did you feel when he told you about me?' I asked now.

'You could have bowled me over with a feather,' was his reply. 'I'd always believed him to be a pillar of probity.' And I believed him. 'I suppose it was like confessing his sins before he died,' he added.

Then we arrived at his place. He had the whole ground floor of a large, Georgian house and I looked around curiously. It was clearly a bachelor pad. There were no signs of a feminine influence on the place, except for a couple of large photos of a young girl sitting on top of a grand piano in the living room. 'Is that your daughter?' I asked.

'Yes,' he replied as he busied himself making coffee in the adjoining kitchen.

'She's pretty. Do you get to see her often?'

'Not as often as I'd like,' he replied. 'She lives with her mother and her new husband in Scotland now.'

He came back in with the coffee and a tray of biscuits and we chatted some more about himself and his family. I found him very easy to talk to and really hoped we would turn out to have the same genetic inheritance. Then I left after he'd called me a taxi, and went home.

The following week seemed to drag interminably but at last the weekend came and I sat by my phone at home waiting for the phone call. "The moment of truth", as I thought of it. But when it finally came, I was in the bath and missed it but it was picked up by my answer phone. I played the message back and listened carefully.

'This is the hospital calling Annabelle. Could you ring us back, please?' was all it said.

I did so immediately and the same nurse replied. 'Oh yes, Annabelle. Thank you for getting back to us. The results of the test are positive so we can confirm that Michael and yourself had the same father.' Just like that! I thanked her profusely and asked her whether Michael had been told yet. Yes, she said. So I hung up and excitedly called him.

'I thought it would be you,' he said. 'It's good news, isn't it?'

'The best,' I said. 'I think we should celebrate. Let me take you out this time.' And he laughed and said okay. So I booked a table at the best restaurant I knew in town just off St James' for that evening. Then I rang him back with the arrangements and he said he'd meet me there.

That evening I dolled myself up and went by taxi to the restaurant. He arrived shortly after me and we were escorted into the restaurant by the head waiter, who probably mistook us for a courting couple. I ordered a bottle of champagne before we'd even sat down and defended myself to Michael saying, 'Well, it's not every day one finds a brother, is it?'

'Or a little sister,' he replied.

The meal was delicious and the time passed far too quickly. We now felt totally comfortable with each other and I realised it was time to tell him about the conversation I'd had with my mother about my parentage.

He was shocked and said, 'That must have been terrible to hear, especially as you were so young.' And I agreed that it hadn't been the most pleasant experience of my life.

When we left, with me a bit tipsy, we kissed each other on the cheek, as I supposed brothers and sisters did everywhere, and I went happily home.

And that is how I discovered I had a family, however small, after all.

Chapter 31

After all that excitement, at last I found myself with some time on my hands and I thought of Luigi but, when I rang the escort agency, I was told he'd already set off on his own travelling adventure, as he'd managed to get the money together for it. That really disappointed me at first as I knew I needed a man.

So I decided to go down a route I'd not wanted to go down before and seek out an appropriate dating agency. I knew I needed help with this and asked Sandra, who was back with me now.

'If it's just a man you need, we could go out together and pull a couple,' she suggested.

It sounded like an attractive proposition at first, but then I realised that it wasn't just a man I needed; it was the permanent company of a man. This was a very surprising realisation when I came to consider it, more like a revelation, in fact. I had never envisioned myself being permanently hitched up with one person but I felt I was now ready for such a dramatic change as I had certainly matured a lot over the past few years. Like so many other women throughout history – and maybe even some men too – I now craved some security and stability in my life and didn't feel I was selling out my feminist principles to find them any way I wanted. So I regretfully turned down her offer and asked her to find a suitable agency for somebody like myself.

'There *is* nobody like you,' she said and we both laughed.

But, as usual, she came up trumps and found me a discreet but expensive agency based in Mayfair. I had to go along for a personal interview before they'd accept me on their books, so one Saturday morning I put on some of my best clothes and jewellery, did my make-up more carefully than usual and took a taxi over to their offices. It was a very plush place with a perfectly made-up mannequin of a receptionist who asked me to wait. So I sat there reading one of the glossy fashion magazines on display.

After a short time, I was called into an office and was confronted by a lady who could have just stepped out of one of their magazines' pages. She made me feel positively dowdy but I didn't care. I just wanted help finding somebody compatible. She asked me lots of questions, some of them, I thought, quite intrusive, like: 'Have you got any sexually transmitted diseases?' although I answered them all as honestly as I could, and she carefully noted down the answers on a long form in front of her and when she'd finished, she sat back in her chair and examined me closely.

'Did I pass?' I asked with an attempt at levity.

'Oh, yes,' she replied seriously in her posh voice. 'You are exactly our sort of customer.'

'Good,' I said. 'So what happens next?'

'Now you will be left alone to scrutinise details of some of our males who, like you, are looking to find someone compatible.' And she took me next door where there was a computer, typed in some instructions to "narrow the field", as she put it, and then left me. I was feeling rather nervous at this stage and wondered if I could actually go through with it. But I looked at her suggestions on the screen and finally came up with two guys who I thought I might like to meet. They were both quite a bit older than me and lived in London. I told the lady, who was waiting outside, my choices and she said that they would be informed of my interest and she'd ring me sometime later that week to arrange meetings with them if, indeed, they wanted to meet me. She'd give me their phone numbers if they agreed.

'Make sure it's somewhere public,' she warned me. Then she asked if they could take a photo of me for their files and I agreed to this. It only took a few minutes.

I left her office, feeling that I had now done something irrevocable, and went home to await her phone calls. It was the following Wednesday before I heard from her about the first guy, a chap called Robin, who I rang and who sounded nice on the phone. We arranged to meet up in the bar of a large hotel in the centre of the city on Friday evening. Then on Thursday I had another phone call from her about the other guy I'd chosen, whose name was Richard, and he also sounded like a reasonable sort, so I arranged a meeting with him too on that Saturday evening. I wasn't sure what would happen if I liked them both equally, it occurred to me after I'd done this. I couldn't string two guys along at the same time, could I? It was against my principles. But I knew I just had to go with the flow and see what happened.

So I went straight from the office on Friday after work to the hotel where I'd arranged to meet Robin, and recognised him at once from his picture in the files. He greeted me politely and we exchanged chit-chat while he bought me a drink. Then we went over to a vacant table where we sat down.

'Have you done this often?' I asked.

'Often enough to know that there are very few ladies out there who attract me enough to want to form a relationship with them or, indeed, who'd be willing to put up with me,' he said.

I admired his honesty, although his tone seemed a bit off, a bit whiney. Then he asked me to tell him a little about my work. I felt a bit like a prospective applicant being interviewed for a job but I told him anyway, without mentioning the fact that I was very wealthy indeed. I didn't want that interfering with the social niceties. Then I asked him about his own job. I knew from reading the details in his file that he was an actuary and I was genuinely interested, never having met one of these before. I knew they were very highly paid and dealt with statistics, setting the rates for everybody's insurance, for example, but that was about it. However, he prevaricated and just said it was boring but useful. So I dropped the subject, asking him instead if he'd ever been married.

'I've never had the time,' he said.

'So no kids, nothing secret in your background that I should know about?' I said, feeling like an interviewer myself now.

'No, nothing. Sometimes I wish I had. It might make me more interesting,' he said and I felt sorry for him, although the answer seemed to have been rehearsed.

The conversation dried up for a few seconds after that but he picked it up again with an important question, asked, however, much too soon.

'Do you think that you and I could make a go of it?' he said almost pleadingly, and I was put off again by his tone.

I felt like saying, 'If you're that desperate for a woman, why don't you just look at the numbers scribbled in every public phone box and ring one of them?' But I was polite and said, 'I'm not sure, Robin. We'll see.' And soon after that I left him sitting there, morosely finishing his drink. I genuinely felt sorry for him but I knew he wasn't right for me and mentally scrapped the idea of another meeting with him, waiting impatiently instead for the following evening when I was to meet Richard.

I knew he was a divorced artist and expected him to be very different from Robin. I'd done a bit of research on him and knew also he was successful, having his works displayed in many of London's top galleries. We'd arranged to meet in his local pub where, he'd told me, he felt safe, which had made me smile over the phone, so I dressed down for the occasion, wearing jeans and a blouse with no jewellery with a long, good coat over the top. When the taxi dropped me off, I went in and was almost overwhelmed by the din of a rock group coming from the back of the pub, but I saw Richard immediately sitting at the bar, nursing a pint of beer. He had long, dark, wavy hair with an ear stud and was wearing old jeans and a smock of some kind and I thought he looked very sexy and artistic. I watched him for a few seconds bantering with the bar maid and then went up to him, held out my hand and introduced myself, shouting to make myself heard.

'Sorry about the racket,' he shouted back. 'Let's go somewhere quieter.'

He led me out back into the garden area of the pub, which was almost empty – it was quite a chilly evening – and it was indeed much quieter there although I could still hear the group playing inside. 'What would you like to drink?' he asked.

'A pint of whatever you're having,' I said.

He grinned, saying, 'A girl after me own heart. Won't be a mo'.' He dashed back inside, reappearing almost immediately holding a foaming pint mug of beer and his own half empty one.

'So, do you come here often then?' he asked with a cheeky grin which reminded me a bit of John – and Luigi!

'No, but you do, I gather,' I said and he grinned again.

It broke the ice and we started chatting about anything and everything. He was a good conversationalist and I enjoyed talking to him. But then after a while I knew I had to ask some more serious questions so I said in a lull, 'Tell me about your wife, Richard.'

He looked at me and replied, 'Oh, getting personal now, are we?'

I blushed, but said, 'I'd like to know more about your past, if that's okay with you.'

'I'll tell you about my past if you tell me about yours,' he said. And I nodded. So he went on to explain how his wife had left him ten years before with their baby daughter when he was still a struggling artist, to shack up with an older man, who, she said, could give her the kind of security she needed. He added wistfully, 'I still miss the baby.'

'Don't you ever get to see her?' I enquired.

'No. They emigrated to Australia and she's made it very clear that she doesn't want to ever see me again. Now tell me about you,' he said, abruptly changing the subject. So, I don't know why, but I opened my heart to him and told him all about my appalling childhood at the hands of my mother and, when I'd finished, I felt like crying. But he held my hands gently in his and said, 'Well then. We're both damaged goods, aren't we?' and he said it in such a kindly fashion that I really did start crying.

'I'm sorry,' I sniffled.

'Oh, there's no need to apologise,' he said. 'I'm well aware that women can cry at the drop of a hat.' But he grinned as he said it and I managed a wan grin back.

'I'd like to see you again,' he said.

I replied, 'Me too.' So we arranged to meet again at his studio in a week's time. Then I went home feeling emotional but happy.

We met on a few more occasions and the simple truth of the matter is, we fell in love. I didn't actually sleep with him until we'd both professed our love for each other, which really surprised me, but when we finally did, the sex was terrific. I asked him afterwards why he'd gone to the dating agency in the first place when he could probably have had the pick of any girl in London and he said, 'I wanted to find somebody special – like you,' and that earned him an extra big cuddle.

I knew he was the man for me when I finally and hesitatingly told him about my fortune and he said he'd known about it all along and didn't give a stuff about it – he was independently wealthy himself. It was me he wanted, not my money.

Soon after this, I moved out of my tiny rented flat and into his capacious house in Hampstead where he both lived and worked, with his studio on the top floor.

Chapter 32

Meanwhile, back at the office, I'd finished writing my report for the board and had delivered it at the annual AGM. I only talked about the business implications of the trip, omitting all reference to the other things we had done, and it went down very well. Afterwards, a lady director congratulated me and said that it would be a good speech to give to senior managers of other big companies. I thanked her although, actually, I'd already thought of that myself.

But not long after this I had to deal with a serious crisis at work, which I found very distressing. One day Chris, my chief accountant, came in looking even more lugubrious than usual and said, 'I'm afraid I've got some very bad news for you, Annabelle.'

Then he fidgeted for a while until I told him to just tell me. He went on to say that he'd been monitoring the account which had had the money disappear from it carefully, as the external auditors had recommended, and had recently noticed a large withdrawal from it, which hadn't been authorised. Then he fidgeted some more before he added, 'And I'm afraid I know who took the money.'

'Who was it, Chris?' I asked, my heart sinking.

'I'm afraid it was Simon,' he said very quietly, looking down at his shoes.

'What!' I screamed. 'That's impossible!'

'I've got the evidence right here,' he said, producing a thin folder from behind his back.

'Show me,' I commanded. He took a few sheets of paper out of the file, laying them on my desk. I looked at them closely. The first couple of pages showed the company bank account and movement within it over the past few weeks and I immediately focussed on one item which had been highlighted. It showed a withdrawal of £145,000 and the date it had been withdrawn. Then I looked at the final sheet and saw it was a copy of a bank withdrawal form, signed by Simon, showing exactly the same amount withdrawn by him on the same day.

'I had to use a forensic accountant, who works hand-in-glove with the banks, to get hold of the withdrawal form, but he told me that it had all been done very amateurishly and involved little work on his part. He also said that it was now your duty to inform the police,' Chris said now.

I was truly shocked by this revelation and wailed, 'But why? Why did he do this?'

'I have no idea but I know he's three months behind with his mortgage payments. I thought I'd better bring it to you straight away. Nobody else knows about it,' Chris said uncomfortably.

'Okay. Thank you, Chris. I'll deal with it. Leave the papers with me,' and he left.

I slumped back in my chair and thought, why did he, of all people, betray me? I've trusted him absolutely.

But then I thought back to something Sandra had said some while before along the lines of, 'I don't know if you've noticed but Simon's been acting a bit strangely recently. Some days he comes in all elated, but more often than not he seems to be very depressed, although it doesn't seem to take him long to get over it once he's here.'

I remembered being up to my eyes in work at the time and replying, 'Don't worry. It's probably just girlfriend trouble.' And I never followed it up. More fool me, I thought grimly.

I knew I had to get it sorted immediately so I asked Sandra to find Simon and send him to me in about half an hour and I spent that time planning my strategy and turning on the tape recorder in my office, which I normally only used when I wanted to record something I'd otherwise forget.

When he came in, he was his usual happy, smiling self and I wondered if Chris could have made a mistake. 'What can I do for you, boss?' he asked.

'You can tell me if you stole £145,000 from a company account for a start,' I replied tersely. I saw him tense up in his chair at my words and I lost eye contact with him.

Then I saw him pull himself together and, with a tremendous effort of will, he said, 'That is completely absurd.' But he still wouldn't meet my eyes.

'I'm afraid I don't believe you,' I said. 'Look at me directly and swear on whatever you hold most sacred that you didn't do it.'

But he couldn't and scrunched up in the chair and started crying. Through his tears I heard him mutter, 'You have no proof of this ridiculous allegation.'

I found his crying embarrassing but said sternly, 'Your tears are proof enough for me and, if you want more proof, I have it on paper too.' I passed him the papers Chris had given me. He leaned forward and glanced at them before collapsing back into his chair again. 'But I would really like to know why you did it? Don't we pay you enough? Why didn't you come to me the moment you got into difficulties? I could have sorted something out,' I said.

And then he folded completely and said piteously, 'I'm a gambler, Annabelle. That's what I do in my free time. And I got myself into serious debt with some very bad people who threatened to do all kinds of nasty things to me unless I paid them back. I *couldn't* tell you about that!'

I gasped. That was something I'd never expected. 'No, I guess you couldn't,' I said as sympathetically as I could. 'But I hope you see what an impossible situation you've put me in. I can't keep you on but, on the other hand, I don't want to have to report you to the police, which I know would be the right and proper thing to do.'

'Why can't you keep me on?' he pleaded, whining. 'I promise I'll reform and pay you back the money over time.'

'No, Simon,' I said firmly. 'That won't work and you know it in your heart of hearts. I have decided to write off the money as severance pay to you and I want you to clear your desk now and leave the building.'

I thought he was going to get onto his knees and beg me to keep him on but, with the remains of his dignity, he just said, 'As you wish, Annabelle,' and got up from his chair.

'Oh, and one more thing, Simon,' I said. 'I have taped this conversation and, if you cause me any more trouble at all, I will not hesitate to send the tape and the other proof to the police. Do I make myself clear?'

He hung his head in shame and said, 'Yes, Annabelle, and I'm sorry for what I did.' And he left my office by a side door.

That was the last time I saw him and the only time I've ever cried while at work. But then Sandra came in and saw me drying my eyes and said, 'Whatever's the matter, Annabelle? Did Simon upset you in some way?'

'You could say that,' I said grimly, 'but I don't want to talk about it right now, if you don't mind. If you could find Chris for me and ask him to come in for a moment, I'd be grateful.' When he arrived, I told him what I'd decided and some of what Simon had said, but without mentioning the gambling, and he nodded.

'I know how close you two were,' he said.

'If you could just tidy up the loose ends for me, I'd be grateful. And I'm sure I don't have to tell you to keep the whole business under your hat for as long as possible.'

He said, 'Of course,' and left.

That was undoubtedly one of the worst days of my working life. When I shared it with Richard that evening, he gave me a long cuddle and said, 'You poor darling! I couldn't do your job if you paid me a million pounds,' and his words and actions comforted me.

Chapter 33

I have almost reached the end of my story for a reason which shall become apparent shortly. Richard and I got married at the end of that tumultuous year and a couple of years later our only child was born, a boy we named Martin. We asked Peter and Michael to be his joint godfathers and they both agreed as I knew they would, Peter coming down from the frozen north for the Christening. Martin is the apple of both our eyes and is already showing a talent for art like his father. It is now ten years down the line since we got married, and a very happy ten years they've been too. I couldn't have chosen a better partner and every so often I give silent thanks to the agency which put us in touch with each other.

I've continued with the business all this time, although I can't go into the office anymore. I can, however, still work part-time from home. Unfortunately, John left a few years ago to start his own consultancy business, which, by the way, is doing very nicely, and I have asked my board to find my successor for when I have to stop working altogether. I believe they'll do a good job, especially as I've given them a strict list of qualities to look for in the candidates and have recommended a couple of people who are already working for me.

I've managed to get the quota of women in senior positions in the company from about 5% to 35% and I think that's something to be proud of. After Martin was born, I had a well-equipped crèche installed in our headquarters, staffed by professionals, for the pre-school children of my employees to use – and, of course, Martin too – and this quickly started turning a tidy profit after I opened it to other businesses in the area.

As for expanding the company, I've always resisted that, thinking that yet more responsibility was something I didn't want to take on. However, it *has* expanded inevitably but each new acquisition has been very carefully vetted.

But at least I've managed to keep its ethos ethically-minded, which pleases me. There was actually one unintended but beneficial business consequence of this: I discovered that most of the developed countries in the world seemed to be choosing their purchases more carefully, not only looking at cost but at their sourcing as well. They no longer want to be associated with companies which use slave labour, for example, however cheap their products are. The little green circle with the legend inside "ethically sourced" has become a prized asset in the business world and I got in on the ground floor. Many of my own companies have already been given the green circle of approval and their profits have rocketed. I've been working hard to make sure that all the relevant companies I own also have it, getting rid of those which have no chance of making it. It's meant a lot of serious investment but the fruits of it are already starting to show.

I also decided long ago to keep the company in private hands, with me owning 51% of the shares and the rest being shared out amongst my employees. My fondest hope is that maybe some day Martin might be able to take over the reins but, if he doesn't want to, that's fine.

Now for the difficult bit: About a year ago, I was diagnosed with terminal pancreatic cancer and was told that I only had six months to live, so I know I'm living on borrowed time. It's the same illness which killed my father according to Michael, my half-brother, and I just hope and pray that I haven't passed the faulty gene on to Martin. I've tried to be brave about the cancer, although sometimes it's very difficult, but that is why I've been hurrying to finish this account of my earlier life.

Michael has been of enormous help with this job, especially typing for me when I've felt too weak to do it myself and editing out the idiocies. I have based it on my old memory sticks, which I took with me to university, and more recent diaries, and I haven't shown it even to my husband, as he has enough to cope with at present just looking after me. Inevitably, I have had to be selective with my memories, but the ones I have written about are the ones I remember best. I intend to pass these memoirs on to Martin to read when he's twenty-one so he can know more about what his mother was like and, hopefully, so he can avoid making the same mistakes my mother and I made. I hope he's not too shocked by what a sexual being his mother was but it was important for me to include this aspect of my life too.

Since I got married, my life has been a lot more stable, although there have, of course, been ups and downs here too. I don't feel that I've done anything in my life to be really ashamed of and have few major regrets, except possibly that I never got to do the psychology research which I had wanted to do when I was young.

I've enjoyed writing this. It has helped me to put things in perspective when I've been low, but has also helped me to remember the good times. I've prepared my will and think that everything's in order for when I go. So I'll see you all on the other side, wherever that is, especially my darlings, Richard and Martin, one day in the hopefully distant future. That's all then. Goodbye!

About the Author

After twenty years roaming the world teaching English, R. J. Sloane returned to England where he has been based ever since. For the past six years, since he was forced to retire from teaching due to medical reasons, he has been concentrating on writing stories for children and young people, inspired mainly by his two young daughters. This is his first adult novel.

By the same author:

For young children:
An Alphabet of Animal Adventures

For older children:
Back to the Dark Ages
Back to Medieval Times
Back to Joan of Arc
Back to the Sioux in 1876 America
Back to Louis Braille in 1823 France
Forward into the Future
(These six titles form a historical / fantasy series)

Cassandra, the Magic Pony

For teenagers:
Teen spirit

Details of all these titles can be found on his website: richardjsloane.wordpress.com